THE TIDDLING TENNIS THEOREM

THE TIDDLING TENNIS THEOREM

Arthur Hoppe

THE VIKING PRESS NEW YORK

Copyright © Arthur Hoppe, 1976, 1977

First published in 1977 by The Viking Press
625 Madison Avenue, New York, N.Y. 10022

Published simultaneously in Canada by
The Macmillan Company of Canada Limited

LIBRARY OF CONGRESS CATALOGING IN PUBLICATION DATA
Hoppe, Arthur Watterson.
The tiddling tennis theorem.
1. Tennis—Anecdotes, facetiae, satire, etc.
I. Title
GV996.H66   796.34′2′0207   76-51815
ISBN 0-670-71251-5

Printed in the United States of America

Set in Linotron Caledonia

Portions of this book appeared in *Atlantic Monthly*.

This book is dedicated to all those tennis players to whom I have brought joy over the years—and to my partners, too.

"Tennis isn't a matter of life and death—it's more important than that." (A motto of the John Gardiner Tennis Clinic, Sugarbush, Vermont.)

CONTENTS

THE TIDDLING TENNIS THEOREM

THE TIDDLING TENNIS THEOREM

The Tiddling Tennis Theorem, which in the end was to alter so drastically the lives of its advocates, was the product of the peculiar mind of John Doe Roberts. Roberts, who was never addressed by any other name than "Professor," had been the teaching professional at the Tiddling Tennis Club for as long as all but the oldest members could recall. The oldest, Doc Pritchgart, claimed the Professor, then a callow youth, had simply appeared one day following World War II, when the Club's membership had dwindled to 124, and had begun offering free tennis lessons. While the Professor's origins remained a mystery, Doc Pritchgart swore the man was the illegitimate son of a war profiteer and an unemployed cancan dancer. But as Doc Pritchgart invariably owed more than $100 on his bar bill, invariably cheated at dominoes, and invariably denigrated the Professor, whom he loathed, few trusted either his judgment, his recollection, or his veracity.

In any event, the Professor, now in his forties, could be found daily, barring rain, standing by the net of the teaching court, lecturing some aspirant to tennis immortality. He always wore the same yellowing flannel trousers, the same faded windbreaker, the same drooping Panama hat that shaded his thin, weathered features and surprisingly bright, deep-set brown eyes, and held the same (Doc Pritchgart contended) unlit cigar between his large, clenched teeth. Two factors distinguished the Professor from every other tennis instructor in the country. One was his unorthodox teaching methods, which he claimed were based on the Tiddling Tennis Theorem. He would begin each half-hour lesson, for which he now charged ten dollars, by removing from his pocket a stack of yellow cards. On each was printed a different maxim. These were known collectively as "Roberts's Rules of Order." With great care, he would unwind the rubber band that embraced them and hand the top card to his student. "Kindly commit this to memory," he would say. When the student nodded to signify this task had been accomplished, the Professor would then deliver a fifteen-minute lecture on the meaning and ramifications of that day's maxim. For the remainder of the half-hour, the Professor would stand at the net tossing balls from a shopping cart at his side at his eagerly swinging pupil. Sometimes the Professor would gaze at the sky, sometimes at the ground, and sometimes his eyes would slowly close. Should the pupil be so brash as to inquire how he should hit the ball, the Professor would sigh, pull another yellow card from his pocket, and silently hand it over. This card read: *"It isn't* how *you hit the ball; it's* where."

But what established the Professor's uniqueness as a tennis instructor beyond doubt was that he had never been seen to hit a tennis ball or, for that matter, to hold a tennis racket in his hand. A few disgruntled members, led by Doc Pritchgart, argued that the Professor didn't know *how* to hit a tennis ball and therefore should be fired as a disgrace to his profession. The other disgruntled members (all members of the Tiddling Tennis Club were disgruntled) felt, however, that the proof was in the pudding, and the success of the Professor's brain child— the Tiddling Tennis Theorem—could not be gainsaid.

What was odd about the Tiddling Tennis Theorem was that the Professor steadfastly refused to divulge its nature. When pressed to the extreme, he would respond gruffly, "No researcher of repute publishes his findings until they have been proved experimentally. I have not yet had the opportunity to conduct my final experiment." Most of his students merely accepted the existence and workings of the Tiddling Tennis ,Theorem on faith, taking comfort, as do we all, from the belief they were being guided by a higher law.

The pupil who came closest to cracking the mystery was Miss Martha (Merri) Merribuck, a slender, comely woman with high cheekbones, long black hair, and an inquiring mind. Miss Merribuck had taken up tennis and reassumed her maiden name in her mid-thirties—after a rather messy divorce, her husband having run off with her hairdresser. It was a great personal tragedy. "I've never found anyone else," she would tell her friends with a game smile, "who could do my hair like Tony." When she met the Professor for her first lesson, she cocked her head to one side, grinned up at him, and asked point-blank, "What is this Tiddling Tennis Theorem of yours anyway?"

The Professor looked at her and looked away. "First," he said, obviously discomfited, "you must realize that tennis is a microcosm of life. You erect an obstacle to surmount. You delineate with carefully drawn lines the boundaries of propriety which determine whether an action you have taken to surmount that obstacle is good or bad. Then, driven by a compulsion to humble your enemies and win the admiration of your fellows, you employ all the tactics and stratagems at your command to surmount that obstacle while remaining within those boundaries of propriety. Second, you must compile and analyze Roberts's Rules of Order. Then, and only then, will the Tiddling Tennis Theorem emerge like a lotus from the mud."

"Is it worth it?" asked Miss Merribuck, smiling.

The Professor shrugged. "I have devoted my entire adult life to it," he said, "for whatever that may be worth."

Miss Merribuck looked at him solemnly. "Okay," she said slowly. "I'll play."

The Professor nodded. He ceremoniously untwisted the rubber band from the stack and extended a card to Miss Merribuck. It bore the first, and perhaps most important, of Roberts's Rules of Order: *"The ultimate goal of all tennis players is to become so proficient they will wish to avoid playing tennis with any other tennis player."*

2

THE TIDDLING TENNIS CLUB

The first thing a beginner must learn is not the forehand, the backhand, the serve, or the volley, but how to pick up the ball. —Roberts's Rules of Order

That the Tiddling Tennis Theorem should have evolved within the confines of the Tiddling Tennis Club was assuredly no accident. The Club provided an ideal cultural medium for the growth of this definitive concept. According to the unreliable Doc Pritchgart, it is the twenty-seventh oldest tennis club in the United States. Opened in 1897, it occupies a full square block in the heart of a once-fashionable neighborhood. An early sketch, now hanging over the bar, depicts a pleasant, tree-shaded expanse of lawn dotted by picnickers, a gazebo, two tennis courts, and a small Victorian clubhouse—all encompassed by a low stone wall. As the neighborhood deteriorated over the years, succeeding boards of directors voted to add more stones to the wall. It now towers thirty-six feet straight up from the barren sidewalks of the ghetto that surrounds it. The sole entrance is through an unmarked, iron-grilled glass door, which opens by a buzzer commanded by Miss Agnes, a thin and dour woman who is feared by all but the oldest members. Miss Agnes has been registering guests, dispensing balls and Band-Aids, answering the telephone, and buzzing the buzzer for twenty-eight years. She loathes junior members, germs, and people who don't say "please."

Once inside the grim walls, the contrast offered by the tasteless modern decor is startling. On the verge of bankruptcy during the Depression, begging for members in the 1950s, the Club, thanks to the recent tennis boom, has been blessed with both wealth and prestige. The initiation fee is now $2000 and, even so, new applicants are informed with barely disguised superciliousness that they can look forward to waiting in limbo for no less than seven years. Dues have risen to $28 a month for men and $25 for women. The Club used to offer family memberships, but, with the high divorce rate created by mixed doubles tournaments and the Saturday Night Glittering Tennis Balls, custody fights over which spouse should retain his or her affiliation became too much of a strain, both on the spouses and the Club's directors, who were all too often called upon to adjudicate the disputes. Now, in the likely event of divorce, both spouses retain their individual memberships, and the strain is solely on them. Consequently, while the Tiddling Tennis Club perhaps boasts no more divorced members than comparable clubs of its size, it certainly can claim having more members who are divorced from each other. This sets the ambience.

In its new affluence, the Club has been redecorated three times in the past eight years. This is due to the number of directors' wives who are licensed interior decorators. Although none, so far as the record shows, has ever been paid to decorate an interior, all enjoy the privilege of purchasing bric-a-brac wholesale, and all have certificates attesting to their good taste. Unfortunately, however, each new board of directors is under pressure from between one and four wives to redecorate "this awful mess." The current decor, recently created by Mrs. Herbert (Bootsy) Smeedle, A.I.D., wife of the President, is monochromatic orange on white with "just a hint of Africa" in the Zimbabwe fertility mask that replaced Mrs. James D. (Betsy) Cooper's framed Marimekko fabric over the fireplace. Bootsy and Betsy aren't speaking.

The two-story clubhouse, with bar, lounge, cardroom, and sun deck on top, and the locker rooms and pro shop underneath, bisects the eleven tennis courts. Two of the courts are grass and dirt (with the latter predominating), two are clay, two are Har-Tru, and the remainder have been recently resurfaced in Plexi-Pave. Thanks to the wide variety of surfaces, Tiddling Tennis Club members never *really* lose matches, except on the scoreboard. "Well, actually they beat us six–three, six–two, but there's no question we would have clobbered them on—"grass, clay, Har-Tru, or Plexi-Pave (choose one). All the members, of course, have preferences for a particular kind of surface, preferences which change only if the players are defeated on that particular kind of surface. But what they enjoy most are the endless interesting discussions of what type of shot works best on what type of surface. "No, I'd never use a spin serve on grass." "Personally, I find a chip backhand far more effective on Har-Tru than Plexi-Pave." "Well, I grew up on clay, and let me tell you that a big overhead . . ." What makes these discussions interesting is that the vast majority of members can hit only one type of backhand, forehand, volley, and serve, and therefore employ precisely the same shots—each a desperate attempt to deliver the ball over the net between the proper lines—no matter what surface they happen to be playing upon.

Court one, directly under the floor-to-ceiling windows of the bar and lounge, is traditionally reserved for top players and other exhibitionists. Court eleven, at the farthest, lowest, southeast corner of the grounds, is the teaching court, where the Professor presides. It is bounded on two sides by the Club's towering stone walls and on the other two by a high wooden fence to insure the Professor's privacy. An initial insight into the Tiddling Tennis Theorem can be gained through the first lesson the Professor gives to rank beginners. It hasn't varied by a comma in the past ten years, nor has his delivery, which approaches an uninterested monotone:

"So you have decided to take up tennis. A marvelous decision. You couldn't have chosen a sport with more to offer: concentrated exercise, intellectual challenge, inexpensive equipment, and a new circle of friends who will provide lifelong companionship. Of course, as in all sports, there are difficulties to surmount. The first difficulty you will encounter is that no one wants to play with you.

"Let us now analyze the game of tennis. It consists of hitting a ball back and forth over a net within a rectangle of white lines. While an experienced opponent will be able to hit the ball *forth* with some consistency, you, as a beginner, will be unable to hit the ball *back*. With all *forths* and no *backs,* most of the time will be devoted to picking up balls. Unfortunately, most experienced players find this a desultory way to spend an afternoon. You will find that lifelong friends who play tennis will, on hearing you have taken up the game, avoid you like the plague.

"The answer would seem to be to discover another beginner with whom to play. Nonsense. The other beginner will have such difficulty hitting the ball *forth* that you will be unable to hit *back*. With neither *forths* nor *backs*, twice as much time will be spent picking up balls. You will never improve your game in this fashion. Moreover, as all beginners quickly grasp this phenomenon, they will not wish to play with you anyway. Thus, even at the very beginning, you learn that the way to improve your game is to play with someone better than you. Now please keep in mind that the all-consuming goal of every tennis player is to improve his or her game, no matter how good or bad it may be. This brings us, then, to the cardinal rule of tennis, which you are now prepared to master."

At this point, the Professor places his cigar in his mouth and peels off one of his little yellow cards. It reads: *"No tennis player, no matter what his caliber, wants to play tennis with any other tennis player who is not better than he."*

"Kindly commit this to memory," says the Professor, pausing to allow the pupil to do so. "Excellent. Now you see that the primary art of tennis is not in playing the game, but in arranging a game. At this very moment, millions of tennis players are hitting the ball back and forth over nets between white lines. And precisely half of them wish they were playing with someone else.

"First of all, they are not improving their games. More important, they are handicapping themselves in the critical art of arranging future games. For if they are seen playing with inferior players, superior players with whom they wish to play will identify them with the inferior players with whom they are playing and will never invite them to play. Worse yet, players slightly inferior to the inferior players with whom they are playing will make the same identification and will besiege them with invitations to play. Such a path can only lead inexorably downward to the depths of degradation.

"How, then, do you, a rank beginner, surmount this initial challenge of finding someone with whom to play? Your first step, obviously, is to disguise the fact that you are a rank beginner. This requires the proper equipment, which Miss Agnes will supply to you after our lesson today.

"Meanwhile, we will turn to mastering the essential skills of tennis. Other instructors usually begin with the forehand and the backhand. This is a waste of time. There is no point in learning the forehand or the backhand if you cannot find someone to hit a forehand or the backhand to. We shall therefore begin with picking up the ball. There is no move in tennis that so well classifies the proficiency of a player than the manner in which he picks up the ball. Once you have acquired the proper technique, it will prove invaluable at cocktail parties.

"As you may have noticed at social occasions, such as cocktail parties and the like, tennis players mysteriously gravitate to each other. Once the conversation turns to tennis, as it inevitably will, they begin sniffing and circling, each trying to determine whether the other is superior or inferior and should therefore be challenged or avoided. Unlike golfers, the handicaps of tennis players are known only to God and those with whom they have played. Thus the opening gambit is invariably, 'Where do you play?' You should reply, 'Oh, here and there.' You will then be asked if you have ever played with so-and-so or so-and-so—an attempt to find a mutual opponent to serve as a standard. As you have never played with anyone, this will fail. The only possible ploy remaining is the question, 'How do you pick up the ball?' If you say you bend over and pick it up with your hand, the average player will switch the conversation to the stock market and go look for an ashtray. If you say you lift it up between your racket and the side of your foot, he might conceivably invite you to play mixed doubles. But— ah!—if you coolly announce that you merely tap the ball rapidly with the strings of your racket—dadada-rup!— causing it to leap up into your waiting hand, he will immediately mark you down as a top-flight player and cleverly inveigle you into a match he will loathe. By attending enough cocktail parties, you will rapidly improve your game.

"You should also, of course, play as much as possible on the public courts. As you saunter up to the bench where the players are waiting, it is a simple technique to drop a ball accidentally, lean over, tap it casually with your racket—dadada-rup!—and inquire guilelessly, 'Anyone need a fourth?' Understandably, none of the other three will ever play with you again, but by visiting all the public courts within a fifty-mile radius at staggered hours, you should eventually score your first triumph on the ladder of success: you will be asked to play tennis by a player with whom you would not be caught dead playing. That concludes our first lesson."

Should the pupil be so bold as to ask for a demonstration on the proper method of picking up a ball, the Professor will light his cigar, stare off into space and say, as always, "One learns by doing, not watching. Go practice, practice, practice."

The pupil then repairs to the pro shop to be equipped for battle by Miss Agnes. It is difficult to determine what, if anything, pleases Miss Agnes. Longtime observers of the subtle changes in her eternally grim visage contend that the one aspect of her duties that causes her excruciating, if well-concealed, delight is selling tennis equipment. And this is odd, for she clearly despises tennis and has never played the game. Be that as it may, she has become the Club's leading authority on tennis equipment, and her advice is eagerly sought by the members. It is the only commodity she dispenses ungrudgingly. When the beginner arrives at the pro shop to be girded for the fray, there is even the hint of a gleam, some say, in Miss Agnes's eye.

"Three shirts, three shorts," she says, piling them on the counter like an army quartermaster. "Be sure to put them through the washing machine for at least sixteen or seventeen cycles before wearing them. That's sixty-two-fifty. One pair of leather tennis shoes at twenty-five. All the best players wear leather tennis shoes. Now you'll want this ninety-five-dollar composition aluminum, fiberglass, and wood racket with the steel-belted throat. It's strung with the finest gut, of course, to give you more feel on your touch shots. It's valuable because it's expensive. Carry it around, and everybody'll think you're a good player. And because it's the latest racket on the market, they'll ask you how you like it. Just say, 'Well, it's probably taken a little edge off my drives, but it's sure helped my tennis elbow.' And speaking of tennis elbow, you'll want this three-ninety-five strap to go around your forearm. That shows you have tennis elbow, which proves you've played a lot of tennis and are, therefore, a reasonably good player. Then you'll need this elastic knee bandage to explain, once you get on the courts, why you aren't."

Miss Agnes adds to the pile wrist bands, sweat bands, hats, visors, a warm-up suit, salt pills, a plastic bottle of

Power Grip powder, two pairs of tinted glasses (blue for bright days, yellow for cloudy days), socks, a tennis ball attached to a weighted base by a fifteen-foot-long rubber band for practicing at home in the driveway, a $40.00 leather bag to transport all this equipment, and a $6.95 book entitled *How to Play Tennis*. The beginner generally staggers out of the pro shop some $400.00 poorer but wiser.

While Miss Agnes does well with beginners, most of the lucrative profits from the shop, which enhance her job security, come from her sales to the regular members. Her technique is basically simple: she merely sells them anything they don't already have. For example, when they develop tennis elbow, as most do, she first determines what kind of racket they have been using. If it is wood, she recommends they switch to metal. "It's the only cure," she'll say, shaking her head solemnly. "The stiffness of a metal racket cuts down on the vibrations that are causing the pain." If, however, they are already playing with metal rackets, she will urge them to switch to wood. "Wood's a lot more flexible," she'll explain equally solemnly, "so it absorbs the shock, and that's what hurts." If they already have both wood and metal rackets, she will sell them new models with different grip sizes and weights, either smaller and lighter or bigger and heavier, depending on what they already have. The challenge is endless. For years, she has been working on designs for a pneumatic cannon that will rapidly fire styrofoam balls, so that players may practice in the privacy of their living rooms with only minimal damage to lamps and bric-a-brac.

"They'll sell like hot cakes," she told the Professor, her only confidant. "I'll bet even Doc Pritchgart would have bought one."

Miss Agnes's particular bete noire was Doc Pritchgart. During his extended playing days, now over, Doc Pritchgart, according to Miss Agnes, had purchased precisely two cans of tennis balls from her, the first in 1948. Whether the charge was true or not, there was no question that Doc Pritchgart set a record for others to shoot at when it came to preserving the virginity of a single can of tennis balls. His technique was simplicity itself. On arriving at the court, he would engage another player in conversation until he heard the tell-tale "pssstttt" of a vacuum-packed can being opened. "Oh, no!" he would cry, holding aloft the can he had brought. "Let's open these." But, darn, it would be too late. On the extremely rare occasions when he was out-stalled, he would feign pleasure. "Well, it's about time I got to provide the balls," he would say, rummaging in his bag. On removing the can, he would turn it upside down and examine its naked underside where, in those rugged days before pop-tops, the small metal key to unwind the opening band was affixed. "Doggone it," he would say. "The key's gone. Could I borrow someone's?" As this would require another player's removing the key from his can and handing it to Doc Pritchgart—a mean and petty act at best—the other player had little choice but to respond grudgingly, "Oh, here, it's easier to open mine."

Like the dinosaur, Doc Pritchgart's downfall resulted from his failure to adapt to changing conditions. A good five years after the demise of the Hammertrunk & Snead Manufacturing Company, he was still arriving at courtside with a pristine can of Hammertrunk & Snead tennis balls. This became too much for his long-suffering colleagues in the regular weekly foursome. On a historic Saturday morning they showed up with three keys and no cans. With the expression Rembrandt might have assumed had he been forced to burn the *Nightwatch* to avoid freezing to death in a Dutch winter, Doc Pritchgart slowly twisted the key in the opening band. There was no hiss, and the white balls, when spilled to the pavement, bounced with all the resiliency of wet noodles. It was at this point that a dispirited Doc Pritchgart purchased his second can of balls from Miss Agnes. Many believed the traumatic experience was one of the primary reasons he gave up the game.

But Doc Pritchgart was an exception in Miss Agnes's brilliant career as a purveyor of tennis equipment. Her greatest coup to date, most agree, was the sale in three days of a dozen $50 laminated-bamboo rackets made in Hong Kong that had been cluttering up the pro shop for six months. Her marketing device consisted of a hand-lettered sign, which she tacked on the wall over the unwanted rackets. It read: "FOR LEFTIES." When queried, she patiently explained that these uniquely designed rackets were "heavier in the head and lighter in the handle," and thus admirably suited to "the sweeping strokes that characterize left-handed players."

She would have been most gratified, one suspects, could she have heard President Herb Smeedle, fresh from another defeat on the courts, talking to Doc Pritchgart in the bar a week later. "I have now bought everything there is to buy to improve my game," said Smeedle, staring glumly down at his new left-handed tennis racket, "and it hasn't."

3

FACTIONALISM IN THE
TIDDLING TENNIS CLUB

*It is not whether you win or lose, it is how far you throw your
racket. —Roberts's Rules of Order*

The Tiddling Tennis Club is, unfortunately, split into a
number of overlapping and interwoven factions. The
basic factions constantly in contention are (1) men, (2)
girls, and (3) Ms. Elizabeth (Beth) Follicle, who objects
strongly to the rest of the women members being called
"girls" and to herself being addressed as "Miss Follicle."
It was Ms. Follicle, a slender, exuberant woman of thirty
who favors white-rimmed harlequin dark glasses who
appeared uninvited before an earlier board of directors
meeting, a serious breach of Club etiquette in itself, to
protest vigorously the allotment of $3762.15 for a sauna
in the men's locker room and, in compensation, $89.95 for

a hair dryer in the girl's locker room. When President Smeedle noted that the girls paid three dollars a month less in dues than the men and were thus entitled to fewer amenities, Ms. Follicle swept off her glasses, pushed back her bangs, called him a male chauvinist pig, and predicted that "no good will come of this." She was quite right. The sauna was completed without incident. But the morning after the next Saturday Night Glittering Tennis Ball, Mr. Belomont (Rocky) Brooks, forty-seven, and Mrs. Lurlene (Lee-Lee) Turgin, thirty-eight, were found wedged against one wall in an advanced state of dehydration. Mr. Brooks apparently had been rendered unconscious by a combination of heat, alcohol, and overexertion. As he was a former Ohio State fullback with a playing weight of 218 pounds, Mrs. Turgin had been unable to extricate herself from beneath him, and her somewhat embarrassed cries for help had been muffled by the heavy door. While both recovered within a week, the near tragedy was the talk of the Club, not to mention the Brookses's and Turgins' households. Ms. Follicle, however, was the only member to draw a lesson from the unfortunate incident. "Why wasn't she on top," asked Ms. Follicle, "where she belonged?"

In addition to men and girls, the Tiddling Tennis Club's roster is divided into full members and social members. Social members are entitled to use the small indoor pool, the exercise room, which is virtually always empty, the billiard and Ping-pong tables, the cardroom, and the bar. Particularly the bar. There is no waiting list for social memberships. Social members are eagerly welcomed in the Club, especially if they are heavy drinkers. Most are middle-aged or more, and while a few occasionally swim, they generally confine themselves to bridge, dominoes, and complaints about any proposed improvements to the tennis courts. When court one was resurfaced last year at a cost of $3618.12, the board of directors, to keep the peace, was forced to purchase an $1800 all-purpose Gym-Dandy exercise machine, which no one uses. But as Social Chairman Gladwyn (Gladdy) Hobbs noted at the time, "We social members drink up that much in a week." They certainly try. The girls begin arriving at eleven-thirty in the morning for their daily bridge game and Bloody Marys. By two in the afternoon, most of the elderly bachelors, led by Doc Pritchgart and Gimper Mudge, have taken their seats around the domino tables to shuffle tiles, sip drinks, and foment trouble. It was at their insistence that the Club remained open until ten o'clock to accommodate between four and six of their number. As this required paying a bartender and doorkeeper overtime, it was considered financially unsound. "Even six social members," said President Smeedle privately, "can't drink that much." But the Club, knowing on which side its budget was buttered, had no wish to offend its social members.

Fortunately, there are no racial factions within the Tiddling Tennis Club. This is primarily because the Club has no black members. It does have a Negro member who used to be its colored member. He is a tall, gentle, Harvard Law School graduate in his fifties named George L. (George) Washington. His major goal is to get more young black members into the Club. He now has three on the waiting list. They are no longer as young as they used to be. It is not that any of the members object to having three more Negroes in the Club, "as long," as Doc Pritchgart puts it, "as they are our kind of people."

But the most virulent factionalism is among the tennis players themselves. Nominally, the members are divided into two groups, A players and B players. One would think that A players played with A players and B players with B players. The problem, however, is that there are as many gradations of A players as there are A players and the same holds true for B players. As there are 475 tennis-playing members in the Tiddling Tennis Club, there are thus 475 factions. These range from forty-seven-year-old Noah (Bang) Banger, the former fourteen-year-old state champion, with whom everyone wants to play, to thirty-six-year-old Melissa (Missie) Marshe, with whom no one wishes to play because of her spectacular lack of hand-eye coordination. Over the years, the 475 factions have coalesced into perhaps 50 uneasy coalitions, each bound together by the unfortunate necessity that every tennis player must, like it or not, play tennis with some other tennis player. Members of the same coalition are friendly, open, and hearty with each other in the locker room and bar, and coolly reserved in their contacts with members of any other coalition. Nowhere, not even in nineteenth-century England, has the social order been so firmly established as in the Tiddling Tennis Club. Nowhere have the class lines been so clearly drawn, and nowhere has class snobbery been so rampant. Herman (Pete) Peters, a back-slapping furniture sales-man, for example, would never dream of slapping the back of Judge Alfred C. (Judge) Kopley. This restraint is not due to Judge Kopley's position on the U.S. Circuit Court of Appeals; it is owing to Pete Peters' being a low A player, while the distinguished Judge is merely a high B player. Should Pete Peters become too friendly with the Judge, the latter might overstep the bounds of propriety and commit the unforgivable gaffe of inviting Pete Peters to "hit a few"—a situation that would be embarrassing to all.

It is precisely this sort of contretemps that is the subject of the Professor's second tennis lesson. The Professor invariably insists that a beginning pupil, after learning—dadada-rup!—to pick up the ball, wait a minimum of sixty days before returning for the second lesson.

"One hopes," the Professor commences, after removing the cigar from his mouth, "that you have now learned the rudiments of how to arrange a game. If you have applied yourself, you should now be able to hit the ball not only forth but, on many occasions, back. You are already superior, then, to many other players. Thus, you must now master the second fundamental of tennis, a fundamental that will stand you in good stead all of your tennis-playing life, to wit: how to avoid a game."

Here, the Professor replaces his cigar and peels off another yellow card. It reads: *"All tennis players are invariably off their game."*

"Kindly commit this to memory," he says, pausing to wait for the pupil's nodded signal of compliance. "There is one member of this Club who is eighty-three years old and who has been off his game for three quarters of a century. Please note that whenever a tennis player misses a shot, he will respond in one or more of the following seven manners: one, he will frown, indicating surprise that a player of his caliber could have failed to convert such an easy opportunity into a blistering winner; two, he will curse, indicating his conviction that the gods are arrayed against him for mysterious reasons of their own; three, he will hold the racket up in front of his face in order to examine it, presumably to make sure he remembered to have it strung before carrying it onto the court; four, after hitting a ground stroke into the net or fence, he will freeze into immobility at the end of his follow-through in order to demonstrate his classic form and show that the blame, therefore, lies with the elements, fate, or anyone in the vicinity but himself; five, he will clutch his elbow, shoulder, wrist, knee, or whatever part of his anatomy it is that is currently causing him suffering, to show that if he had not been in agonizing pain, he would have executed a perfect shot (conversely, a player who does execute a perfect shot *never* suffers pain, no matter how disabled he may be); six, he will drop his racket with a clatter to show his disgust with the way he is playing, his partner, his opponents, the game of tennis in general, or life itself; or seven, he will simply hurl his racket at the net, fence, or sky. This suggests he is angry.

"In any one of these cases, it matters not a whit that the player has missed precisely the same shot on several thousand previous occasions. If he were on his game, he would have made it. As every player invariably misses dozens of shots in every match, every player is, *ipso facto,* invariably off his game. The underlying cause for this phenomenon is not difficult to unearth."

Now the Professor peels off a second card: "*Every tennis player honestly and sincerely believes that he is a far better tennis player than he actually is.*"

"I assume," continues the Professor when the pupil has memorized this maxim, "that you have observed the framed admonishment over the bar which states, 'Members will please refrain from challenging superior players.' I will concede that no member would dare commit such a breach of etiquette. The problem arises with the lesser player who believes he is better than he is and thus also believes he is as good as you—you who naturally believe you are better than you are. The danger of accepting the challenge of this lesser player lies not only in the damage it will do to your social standing to be seen playing with him, but in the threat that he may defeat you if you are off your game. And, as you are always off your game, this is a distinct possibility.

"On the surface, the solution to avoiding a game would appear simple. You merely offer some polite excuse, such as: 'Thank you, I'd love to play if I hadn't just broken my left leg in three places above the knee.' This would indicate you didn't wish to play. But you do wish to play. You wish to play with someone else. And should you subsequently inveigle a superior player into a match, the inferior player you avoided would be fully justified in shouting from the sidelines as you reach up to smash away an easy lob, 'Leg feeling better?' This may cause you to miss the shot and put you further off your game, which you are already off.

"Therefore, it is best to hedge. An excellent place to practice hedging is the Club lounge on Saturday and Sunday mornings. You will discover that it is always crowded with members eyeing each other uneasily, whispering in corners, or if they are the passive type, staring stoically out the window, hoping against hope that three better players will desperately need a fourth. Every invitation is, of course, a gamble. Should you invite this slightly inferior player to make a fourth? Or should you delay, hoping that a slightly superior player may wander in? But if one doesn't, you may meanwhile lose the slightly inferior player and be forced to settle for a decidedly inferior player, much to everyone's disgrace. Conversely, should you accept an invitation from a slightly inferior player or delay in hopes a slightly superior player will wander in and . . . But you can readily see the exciting challenges the art of avoiding a game offers.

"Let us turn to the techniques. How do you avoid an invitation from an inferior player? This depends solely on how inferior he is. If he is only slightly inferior, and you may wish to play with him if no one better wanders in, the proper response is: 'Thank you, I'd love to play, but I already have a game, I think.' The advantage of hedging is that as the morning wanes, and you grow increasingly desperate, you can approach him with the happy news that the game you thought you had has failed to materialize, thank God, because you would much rather play with him. No harm done. But if the invitation is extended by a decidedly inferior player, one with whom you would not be caught dead playing either now or in the foreseeable future, you can afford to be—nay, you must be—brutally dishonest. 'Thank you,' you should say coldly, as you sit there in your tennis whites twirling your racket, 'but I'm not playing today.' You should then arrange any game you are able to arrange, so that the decidedly inferior player will see that you are, too, playing today. He will never have the temerity to approach you again. Should you be tempted to be soft-hearted, remember that you are sternly disciplining him for his own good." Here again, the Professor peels off a card from his seemingly inexhaustible supply: *"No tennis player can enjoy the happy camaraderie that tennis offers until he has learned his proper place."*

"You have now mastered the two basic principles upon which all tennis matches depend," concludes the Professor: "how to arrange a game and how to avoid a game. All that remains is to learn how best to hit the ball over the net between the white lines. You will find this relatively simple."

4

TIDDLING TENNIS
CLUB AFFAIRS

*The proper method of playing mixed doubles is to hit the ball
accidentally at the woman player as hard and as accurately as
possible. —Roberts's Rules of Order*

The Professor's antecedents remained a mystery, despite
the best efforts of the curious Doc Pritchgart to unearth a
clue. The name of John Doe Roberts appeared neither in
the telephone directory nor on the voting rolls. The
frustrated Doc Pritchgart went so far as to devote an
entire day at City Hall to poring through musty records.
He could not find a birth certificate, a marriage license, a
property tax filing, or even a parking ticket that could be
ascribed to the Professor. Once he went so far as to ask
slyly, "Don't you think, Professor, your home telephone
should be on file with Miss Agnes in case of an emergency?"

"I don't contemplate one," replied the Professor.

Doc Pritchgart gave no consideration to questioning the Professor's friends in the Club, primarily because the Professor had none. The latter would arrive each morning promptly at eight and stride directly to the teaching court for his first lesson, head bowed over pen and notebook, which absorbed his full attention. Should a member say, "Good morning," he would nod. Should a member say, "Nice day, Professor," he would nod and reply, "Yes." He invariably lunched alone on the stool at the farthest end of the bar, studying his notebook and occasionally making a painstaking entry, his concentration discouraging any attempt at conversation. Promptly at four-thirty, following his last lesson, he would make his way out the grilled front door and vanish into the ghetto.

"I don't think he *has* a private life," President Smeedle said in response to the growing number of Doc Pritchgart's complaints on the subject.

"Well, whatever he has," said Doc Pritchgart, "it's damn sure private."

The blossoming of the Professor's relationship with Miss Merribuck, therefore, was the chief topic of conversation about the Club for a full two weeks. It was not that even the most gossipy suspected the two of having an affair; it was that Miss Merribuck suddenly became the one member the Professor didn't avoid. She had taken a dozen or so lessons from him and had, as a result, reached the plateau of an adequate B player. At that point, she informed the Professor she had decided to cancel further instruction.

"Certainly," said the Professor. "I'll scratch your name from my appointments list."

"Don't you want to know why?" asked Miss Merribuck.

"Certainly," said the Professor without much interest.
"It isn't you, you know. I think you're marvelous."
"Thank you."

"It's just that I've found a pleasant, compatible group to play with, and I don't see any reason to get any better, do you?"

The Professor put down his notebook and looked up at her oddly. "What?" he said.

She smiled. "Well, I'm never going to get to Wimbledon, am I? So why should I try to improve? If I improve, I'll have to go through all that dreadful business of avoiding the friends I'm playing with now while I try to worm my way into a better group, won't I? Then, if I improve even more, I'll have to abandon them and look for an even better group. And so on. I simply don't see the point of it all, do you?"

For the first time in memory, the Professor smiled at a pupil. "Miss Merribuck," he said, "you are the only student I have ever had who took that approach. Please permit me to buy you a drink in the lounge."

Miss Merribuck thus made history by becoming the first member of the Club for whom the Professor had ever purchased a drink. This, in turn, led to further intimacies. The following day, Miss Merribuck approached the Professor on his stool at the far end of the bar and suggested he join her at a table by the plate-glass windows overlooking court one for lunch. After a moment's hesitation, he agreed. From then on, following her regularly scheduled ladies' doubles matches on Tuesday and Thursday mornings, they would eat together, the Professor commenting dryly on the tennis being played below, and Miss Merribuck, as was her wont, eagerly asking questions. The Professor's lunch, provided gratis by the Club in return for his services, consisted invariably of a double martini over ice with a lemon twist. For years, the Professor's free lunch had been a source of contention among the members. One faction, led by Mrs. Cooper, held that a double martini was a bar item and not a food item, and therefore was unacceptable as a free lunch. The other faction noted, however, that Mrs. Cooper, herself, lunched exclusively on two Bloody Marys and was hardly the one to criticize the Professor's menu selections. This argument angered Mrs. Cooper. "Bloody Marys have tomato juice in them," she would respond. "And that's nourishment." Efforts to make peace by persuading the Professor to switch to Bloody Marys were to no avail. A compromise was reached when he agreed to chew on the lemon twist daily, and there the matter rested uneasily.

The growing alliance between the Professor and Miss Merribuck created more surprise than suspicion, primarily, as Mrs. Nancy Jo (Cuppie) Pfluger put it, "It's really just too impossible to imagine the Professor having an affair with anyone." The fact that Miss Merribuck was divorced, and therefore theoretically on the prowl, had little bearing on the question. First of all, she was well liked. She was well liked by the women members because she scrupulously avoided dancing cheek-to-cheek with anyone else's husband. The men universally admired her, as she flirted impartially, if jocularly, with them all. Furthermore, being divorced was not only acceptable within the group, it was commonplace. Any fleeting interest in the alliance between Miss Merribuck and the Professor was quickly buried in the eruption of excitement over the forthcoming battle for the Dee Cup.

When Miss Agnes pushed her buzzer unlocking the barred doors of the Tiddling Tennis Club, the first sight to greet the visitor was the Club's large walnut-and-glass trophy case. In it were two shelves. On the lower was a silver platter inscribed, "To Our Beloved Sam, in Appreciation of Twenty Years of Loyal Service"—Sam being the faithful Chinese retainer who had presided over the bar and lounge at considerably below the minimum wage and considerably above the maximum hours set by state law ever since his illegal arrival from Hong Kong. After the brief presentation ceremonies four years before, it was decided to place the platter in the locked trophy case where Sam could admire it daily, and still avoid the temptation to pawn it. Unbeknownst to the Club at the time, Sam had been a member of the Trotskyist Workers' Party for the past decade and more. At cell meetings he showed little interest in discussing the Marxist dialectic, but no one was more enthusiastic than he when it came to shouting the party's slogan, "Death to the bosses!"

On the upper shelf was the Tiddling Tennis Club's most prized possession, the permanent trophy donated thirty-four years earlier by the late Henderson F. Dee. The trophy was an inverted, swelling cone of ribbed silver some seven inches high. From the upper lip a curling band of silver projected to either side. For thirty-three years, the Dee Cup, as it was fittingly known, had been awarded annually to the winner of the Labor Day tournament between the Tiddling Tennis Club and its arch-rival, the suburban Crestmarsh Racquet Club, a name suggesting a swamp on top of a hill. According to its brochures, however, "The Crestmarsh Racquet Club offers the finest of tennis facilities under the direction of Rodney (Whizzer) Whitman, the former Junior National Clay Court Doubles Champion, as well as an Olympic-size pool, an eighteen-hole putting green, and the beautiful Stardust Lounge for weddings and catered parties—all located in a sylvan setting only twenty minutes from downtown." By helicopter. The tournament consisted of one men's doubles, one men's singles, and one mixed doubles match. In recent years this has sparked a vehement annual protest from Ms. E. Follicle, who unsuccessfully demanded the inclusion of women's singles and doubles matches as well. "Why aren't women equal to men?" she cried out at the annual membership meeting two years ago. The response of the directors was summed up by Doc Pritchgart: "Damned if we know," he said.

But the affair was eagerly looked forward to each year by members of both clubs. What they particularly looked forward to was the Labor Day Eve No-Host Cocktail Party, Buffet Supper & Mixer, given alternately by the Tiddlingers and the Crestmarshians. The Mixer offered members of each club the opportunity to renew old acquaintances and get in trouble once again with the spouses of the other club. Indeed, over the years, the mixers had produced a number of wife-and-membership swaps—the rule being that the wife who renounced her old husband also renounced her old club and went to the head of the waiting list of her new husband's club. This naturally served to increase the rivalry. The Crestmarshians, a hard-driving, competitive lot, coached in traditional fashion by Whizzer Whitman, now in his sixties, invariably won the singles match, but the Tiddlingers generally did better in the two doubles matches, thanks to the theories of the Professor. To date, the Tiddlingers had won sixteen tournaments, the Crestmarshians had won sixteen tournaments, and one tournament had ended in what was euphemistically termed "a mutual default." This occurred the previous year at the Crestmarsh Club. The Crestmarshians had won the men's singles, as usual, and the Tiddlingers the men's doubles. The climactic deciding match was therefore the mixed doubles. Unfortunately, it ended before it began, when Mrs. Bonnie

Ellis Hatchbee, accompanied by her new husband, walked on the court to discover that her female opponent was Mrs. Mary-Jane Hatchbee Ellis, accompanied by her new husband. This resulted, progressively, in one snide remark, three shouted accusations, a hair-pulling contest, two fistfights, and a shattered plate-glass window in the Stardust Lounge a good hundred feet from the court, which, as the Professor later commented, "proves there is hardly any limit to how far a determined player, when he puts his mind to it, can throw his racket."

As a result of this unpleasantness, the directors of the two clubs voted to break off relations and terminate the annual tournament once and for all. The question arose, however, as to the disposition of the Dee Cup. The Tiddlingers contended it was theirs, on the grounds they had won it the year prior to the mutual default; it therefore presently rested in their trophy case; and possession was, after all, nine points of the law. In an irate letter of rejoinder (telephone communication was no longer possible), the Crestmarshians noted that the tournaments were tied at sixteen all; that the honorableness of tennis players was inherent in the nature of the game; and that if the Tiddlingers did not see it their way, legal proceedings would be undertaken. Fortunately, cooler heads prevailed. To avoid a bitter custody fight in court, it was reluctantly agreed to play one final Labor Day tournament, the winner to take possession of the Dee Cup forevermore.

The decision was reached in late January. In the succeeding months, the Tiddlingers talked of little else but who should represent them in this crucial final tournament, and who was having an affair with whom, which they never ceased talking about, no matter what. Speculation centered on the mixed doubles team, primarily because this afforded the members the opportunity to combine their two favorite subjects in the same paragraph. It was generally agreed that, following the second divorce of Mrs. Bonnie Ellis Hatchbee, the best mixed doubles team was Bill and Janine Collums. There were no more than a dozen married couples in the Tiddling Tennis Club who still played tennis on the same side of the net and, in most cases, if pressed to designate their marital status, they would have been forced to respond truthfully, "shaky." But the Collumses were the glowing exception. He was a slender, handsome stockbroker in his forties with a deep tan, curly, graying hair, and a hearing aid. Mrs. Collums, a buxom blonde, invariably wore a green visor and a fixed smile. On the court, she chattered constantly. He, once the match began, never looked her way or uttered a word. They had married young, in the days before the women's liberation movement raised its pretty head. Mrs. Collums believed not in sexual equality but rather in sexual togetherness, her somewhat questionable theory being that the more time a couple spent in each other's company, the more permanently their relationship would be cemented. In the early years of their marriage, Collums was flattered by his wife's desire to do whatever he wished to do, and by the way she deferred to him when it came to choosing a trail or picking a camping site. As they grew more affluent, they took up skiing together in the winters and sailing together in the summers, and Collums grudgingly admired his wife's gameness in blizzard and gale. In the tenth year of their marriage, Collums announced he was going to try his hand at duck hunting. He was glumly surprised at what an adequate shot Mrs. Collums quickly became. The following spring, when Mrs. Collums announced one evening at dinner that "all our friends are joining tennis clubs," Collums could do no more than nod resignedly. He had not been converted to the doctrine of togetherness, he had merely been defeated by it. And so tennis, as it must to many marriages, came at last to the Collumses, but theirs it improved. They played together every weekend and on summer evenings, and they never, ever fought. "Such a devoted couple," Melissa Browning Watts Cyznitski, who had two former husbands on the Club roster, commented enviously. "It's really a miracle, don't you think?" The miracle, such as it was, had of course been wrought by the Professor. When the Collumses reported to him for their third lesson, he looked them over carefully and permitted himself a rare nod of approval. "I can see," he said, "that you two have great potential. By now you have presumably acquired the rudiments of the two most important challenges of tennis: one, how to arrange a game and two, how to avoid a game. Most teachers at this point would turn to how to play the game, beginning with singles and progressing to doubles. In my third lesson, however, I concentrate on mixed doubles."

"You mean it's easier to play mixed doubles?" asked Collums with surprise.

The Professor looked at him sadly, stuck a cigar in his mouth, and handed each of the Collumses a yellow maxim that read: "*To achieve flawlessness in the art of tennis arranging as rapidly as possible, confine yourself to mixed doubles.*"

"I don't see—" said Collums, studying the card.

"Keep in mind," said the Professor, "that women generally prefer to play mixed doubles because men are generally better players. Conversely, men, for the same reason, prefer self-flagellation. Here, then, is the ideal situation to exploit when it comes to arranging and avoiding games."

The Professor aimed his cigar at Collums. "For example, an inferior player approaches you in the lounge and suggests you 'hit a few.' Your reply, of course, is: 'I'd love to, but I'm committed to mixed doubles with my wife.' You won't be bothered by him again. Now, then, how do you get a game with a superior player? The answer is sex."

Mrs. Collums blushed. "You mean I should—"

"Exactly," said the Professor. "You should approach the most attractive young lady available in the lounge and invite her to play mixed doubles with you and your husband—if she can find a fourth. She, in turn, will seek out the best male player in the room, married or otherwise. And he, in turn, will be severely torn between her charms and the depressing thought of three sets of mixed doubles. In two cases out of three, sex will triumph over tennis. Thus you will constantly be playing with better players and constantly improving your game. And while it is difficult to estimate how many marriages you will break up along the way, there is no telling how far you can go as a team with your obvious physical assets."

"Well, I guess I am in pretty good shape," said Collums modestly.

"I was referring to your hearing aid," said the Professor. "The problem a married couple faces in playing mixed doubles is that the husband is generally better than the wife. He therefore wishes he were playing with someone else. He consents to play with his wife, however, in order to accumulate marital points. She, of course, senses his condescending attitude, realizes that she is losing marital points and is consequently furious with him before they have reached the court. Once play commences, the situation deteriorates rapidly. He feels superior, not only athletically, but morally, for nobly sacrificing an afternoon to her pleasure. She feels inferior on both counts. In her determination to achieve some semblance of equality, she will miss more shots than she would normally miss. The more shots she misses, the more resentful she grows, and the more insufferable he becomes. Finally, his male ego becomes so boundless that he commits the unpardonable sin of offering her some bit of advice, such as, 'Perhaps if you stood back a foot or so to receive that serve . . .' She, seething, will do as instructed, swing wildly at the ball, relish the sight of it smashing into the net, and turn on him with a snarl: 'If you hadn't told me to stand back a foot . . .' Scenes such as these will lead inevitably to defeat and divorce."

"Bill," said Mrs. Collums nervously, "maybe we should take up hang gliding with the Harrises."

"You are forgetting your husband's hearing aid, Mrs. Collums," said the Professor.

"I can't stand it when he turns me off," she said.

"He won't be turning you off, Mrs. Collums," said the Professor. "He will be turning himself off. I assume, Mr. Collums, that when your hearing aid is off, you not only do not hear but do not speak?"

"That's right," said Collums. "There's no point in saying something if you can't hear the reply. Gets you in all kinds of trouble."

"Exactly," said the Professor. "Therefore, by turning off your hearing aid, you will not only fail to hear her comments to you, but, far more important, you will refrain from making comments to her. Here, then, lies the key to a lasting marriage and an unbeatable mixed doubles team."

Mrs. Collums was still frowning. "I don't know," she said. "I've always felt that the couple who plays together stays together."

"Believe me, Mrs. Collums," said the Professor, "that

adage never has, does not now, and never will apply to mixed doubles."

The Professor then closed out the lesson with his traditional lecture on how to play mixed doubles. "First, the woman player should stand at all times within six inches of the net, her racket protecting her face. This prevents her opponents from hitting the ball in her direction unless the man is an extraordinarily powerful player and an absolute beast.

"Second, once the man has acquired the necessary power and accuracy, he should become an absolute beast. But, after hitting the first possible ball accidentally at the woman player as hard and as accurately as possible and thereby unnerving her for the remainder of the match, he must apologize profusely so that his male opponent, if he has a shred of gallantry in his soul, won't be tempted to retaliate in kind.

"Third, remember that mixed doubles is the only known competitive sport in which, to paraphrase a collo-quialism, nice guys finish first. It is primarily up to the male not only to maintain equanimity on his side of the net but to create dissension on the other. The more considerate he is of his female partner, the more his female opponent will contrast his behavior with that of her male partner, and the more testy she will become. Her testiness, needless to say, will be contagious and will flare into epidemic proportions in direct ratio to how quickly the score mounts against them. No matter how far behind you are in any mixed doubles match, never say die; for if you can cause your opponents to snarl at each other but once, victory is within your grasp.

"Last," said the Professor, concluding his lesson on mixed doubles, "never challenge the rare couple who has a perfect marriage."

After only four years of playing together, the Collumses won the Club's mixed troubles championship, as it is humorously entitled, when the Wembleys defaulted in the third set of the finals. The default was called when Mr. Wembley suffered a nasty scalp wound inflicted by Mrs. Wembley's racket after she missed an easy overhead at the net and he suggested she shorten her backswing.

It was mixed doubles, oddly enough, that further cemented the relationship between the Professor and Miss Merribuck.

"I'm thinking of getting married again," she suddenly confided to him one day at lunch. "Do you think it's a good idea?"

"Certainly," said the Professor, tapping his lemon peel against the side of his glass. "If tennis is, as I believe, a microcosm of life, one should note that the boundaries for doubles are wider than those for singles."

Miss Merribuck nodded slowly. "I know what you mean, I think. Two against the world and all that?" She sipped her coffee. "Do you know? I've never liked singles. I hate it when I lose. I suppose that's normal, isn't it? But I also hate it when I win. I don't know whether it's that I feel sorry for the person I beat or I'm afraid she'll hate me for beating her."

"But you like doubles?"

"Yes. Have you ever thought of getting married?"

"I fear I don't even play singles," said the Professor. "But what's his name?"

"Whose name? Oh, it's Hewlett White. He's really quite nice, I think. But we've only been dating for a couple of months, and I just don't know whether—"

"Does he play tennis?" asked the Professor.

"Yes. I mean he says he does. But he isn't a member of

the Club and we've never played. We haven't even . . . I mean, for God's sakes, we haven't even . . . I mean, you know what I mean."

"I take it you haven't yet consummated your affair."

"Yes. I suppose that's a prerequisite, isn't it? I suppose I can guess how you feel about that, can't I? To be honest, I'm a little old-fashioned myself. But these days, it simply wouldn't do to marry someone you hadn't been to bed with, would it?"

"Why not?"

"Well, how would you know whether you were suited to each other? How would I know what kind of man he was? I've made one mistake, you know. I'd really hate to make another."

The Professor nipped off the end of his lemon peel and chewed it thoughtfully. "Play tennis with him."

"Tennis? What's tennis got to do with anything?"

"I confess my experience is limited," said the Professor, "but I would assume that a gentleman taking a lady to bed would be on his very best behavior—tender, adoring, considerate, and protective. No activity on earth would cast him in a more favorable light."

Miss Merribuck frowned. "I never thought of it that way," she said. "You really do have a point, don't you?"

The Professor nodded, his eyelids half-closed. "I would suggest that you play tennis with him first," he said, "and then go to bed."

Miss Merribuck invited her intended to be her partner in a mixed doubles match the following Saturday. He arrived on time. Miss Merribuck introduced him to the Professor, who found him to be a polite, charming young man with a warm smile and a deferential attitude toward Miss Merribuck which hinted at true and everlasting adoration. Their opponents were to be the Collumses. During the warm-up period, White was the soul of devotion as far as Miss Merribuck was concerned, going out of his way to retrieve balls for her and complimenting her excessively on her ladylike, if not overpowering strokes.

"Are you ready, Merri?" he asked Miss Merribuck.

"Sure," she said.

"We're ready when you're ready, but no hurry," he politely informed the Collumses.

"Go ahead and serve," said Collums, reaching up to flick off his hearing aid.

"Why don't I serve first?" said White, taking the balls from Miss Merribuck.

"Okay," she said.

His first serve to Mrs. Collums was, as prescribed in social mixed doubles, a gentle ball to her forehand. Mrs. Collums lofted it back over Miss Merribuck, who just managed to reach up and tick it with her racket. White frowned. "If you can't reach them, dear, perhaps it's better if you leave them for me," he said.

"I know that," said Miss Merribuck.

His first serve to Collums was a boomer that boomed a good twelve feet out. His second was a patty-cake, which Collums sent whistling back between Miss Merribuck and the in-rushing White.

"I thought I might tick it," explained Miss Merribuck.

"You really have to cover your side of the court," said White.

By the time they were down four–love, White was serving as hard as he could to Mrs. Collums' backhand. He was also bashing them at her at the net without bothering to apologize, meanwhile offering Miss Merribuck a great deal of helpful advice. "Try tossing the ball higher," he would say after she double-faulted once. "Let me check that grip," he would say when she missed a backhand. "You've simply got to switch on those," he would say after she flubbed an easy overhead. As the score mounted against them, his face grew more red and his calls more questionable.

"Good serve," said Miss Merribuck after netting one of Mrs. Collums' offerings to her backhand.

"Sorry, I thought it was out," said White grimly after having waited to see if Miss Merribuck would successfully return it. "Why don't you play two?"

The final results were eighteen straight games for the Collumses and a broken romance for Miss Merribuck.

"Well, back to the hunt," she told the Professor at lunch the next Tuesday.

"I'm really terribly sorry I interfered," said the Professor. "I never do, you know."

"No, I'm glad you did, she said. "Imagine being married to a man like that. Maybe I'll have to find a man who doesn't play tennis." She smiled. "But then how would I find out what he was really like?"

"Well, it's not quite as effective a test," said the Professor thoughtfully, "but you could always go camping in the rain with him."

Miss Merribuck laughed. It was the first time that the Professor had caused any member of the Club to laugh. The number of historic firsts Miss Merribuck was compiling with the Professor were to have, it is now generally believed, a drastic effect on who would forever retain possession of the Dee Cup.

5

TIDDLING TENNIS
CLUB TOURNAMENTS

There is no more accurate test of your tennis ability than the challenging game of singles. Therefore, avoid it at all costs.
—Roberts's Rules of Order

In addition to the mixed troubles tournament, the Tiddling Tennis Club offers, for the pleasure of its members, annual men's and women's singles and doubles tournaments. All tournament matches commence precisely on time, one hour late. The reason for this is that the Professor, in one of his advanced lessons, instructs his pupils to be invariably late for tournament matches in order to unnerve their opponents.

"You should arrive breathlessly apologetic with some simple excuse," he says, "the most effective is that you completely forgot you had a match. The toll this takes on your opponent—who has devoted several days to plotting strategy, practicing strokes, and otherwise reaching a pinnacle of nervous exhaustion—is incalculable."

Unfortunately, most members of the Tiddling Tennis Club had become aware of the Professor's tactics and vied with each other in tardiness. The record was set in his younger days by Doc Pritchgart, who showed up Sunday afternoon for a Saturday morning contest. This so angered his opponent that he hit the fence on the fly with his first serve. Not only did such delays seriously interfere with the orderly scheduling of matches, but Miss Agnes grew increasingly annoyed during tournaments by constant telephone calls from players at home who would ring up to inquire whether their opponents had arrived at the Club. When Miss Agnes became annoyed, it was obvious that drastic measures were necessary. Consequently, the rule that any player more than sixty minutes late for a match automatically defaults has been rigorously enforced ever since. Thus the Professor, whose burden it is to arrange the tournaments, merely schedules all matches one hour earlier than necessary, and all matches, thanks to the reliability of the members, are therefore played precisely on time.

While the doubles tournaments draw a heavy turnout, no more than a score of men, and even fewer women, sign up for the singles tournaments, as very few members of the Tiddling Tennis Club play singles. The Professor, in his fourth lesson, dispenses with the game of singles with the aforementioned maxim. Should his pupil fail to grasp the point, the Professor hands him a second yellow card: *"The advantage of doubles is that no matter whether you win or lose, no one not present knows how you played the game."* He then devotes the remainder of the lesson to a lecture on the unwritten rules of tennis sportsmanship and of how best to take advantage of them.

Those who do play singles at the Tiddling Tennis Club may be divided into two groups: one is composed of hard-driving, fiercely competitive, physical-fitness advocates who, while not precisely ostracized, are viewed as lacking the *élan* of true Tiddlingers, and they take little part in club affairs—political, social, or otherwise. The other group is composed of psychiatrists. The club's membership runs heavily to lawyers, doctors, and brokers of stocks or real estate, but there is also a liberal sprinkling of liberal psychiatrists. No one is quite sure why so many psychiatrists are attracted either to the Club or to tennis. The irreverent F. Whiting Bayswope, the Club's one professional author (*I, Myself, and Me,* Vanity Press, 1965, and "Thoughts on the Metaphysical," *Metaphysical Magazine,* Autumn 1970), contends psychiatrists join the Club so they can write off their whole tab under "advanced professional education," rather than, as most members do, "business entertainment." Whatever the reason, the dozen or more psychiatrists in the Club are among the few members who prefer singles to doubles. (Bayswope claims they are constitutionally incapable of playing games that require cooperation, but he appears biased on the subject.) They also play primarily against each other. One reason is that the other members tend to avoid games with them. "It's bad enough talking to a psychiatrist at a cocktail party," explains Bayswope, "but on the tennis court it's worse. Even I can tell a lot about a man's sanity by the way he plays the game." Another is that the psychiatrists are generally the most temperamental players in the Club. "Join the Tiddling Tennis Club," said Bayswope the other day as he observed Dr. Wolfgang Schmidt, director of the Center for Behavior Control, hurl his racket over the fifteen-foot-high fence separating court six from court seven, "and watch the shrinks blow."

The sight was not unusual. Actually, Dr. Schmidt had hurled his racket over the same fence every rainless Tuesday at approximately 1:25 p.m. for the past six years. The scenario was unvarying. Dr. Schmidt would arrive in the locker room at 12:05 for his Tuesday match with Dr. Pascal Lefkowitz. Both would silently change into their tennis clothes, silently swathe their knees, ankles, and wrists in elastic bandages, and silently repair to court six with three cans of tennis balls. (The extra balls were necessary because of Dr. Lefkowitz's habit—after missing an easy shot—of angrily hitting the first stray ball he could lay his hands on over the wall and into the street.) After seven minutes of silent rallying, Dr. Lefkowitz would spin his racket to determine who would serve first. Dr. Lefkowitz always served first. For no matter whether Dr. Schmidt called "up" or "down," Dr. Lefkowitz would examine the trademark on the butt of his racket handle, shake his head, and begin serving. Dr. Schmidt would retaliate by giving Dr. Lefkowitz a bad call in the first game. Dr. Schmidt would immediately respond with a bad call of his own. By the middle of the first set, any ball within a foot inside the line on either side of the net was grimly gestured out, thus effectively narrowing the dimensions of the field of play. As Dr. Schmidt's temper mounted, he began hitting the peculiar shot that had been named in his honor by the members of the Tiddling Tennis Club. By definition, a "Schmidt" was any ball that cleared the net by no more than twelve inches and then struck the back fence on the fly. Needless to say, the shot was effective only if it could be bounced off one's opponent, and if there was one move that Dr. Lefkowitz had mastered over the years, it was ducking. Thus by 1:25 p.m., the two contestants were down to their last few balls, and Dr. Schmidt had been defeated again by the same score, six–two, six–two, six–two. Over the fence the racket would sail, Dr. Lefkowitz would then break his eighty minutes of silence by commenting, "Nice throw." Dr. Schmidt would reply sullenly, "Next Tuesday?" And the two would trudge silently back to the locker room.

When it came to selecting a champion to represent the Tiddling Tennis Club in the men's singles match, there was, therefore, not much to choose from. "I suppose we'll have to go with Oats again," said President Smeedle with a sigh. While Otis (Oats) Otis III was the scion of a socially prominent family, he was the disgrace of the Tiddling Tennis Club. Financially independent, he had done nothing for thirty-five of his forty-six years but play tennis. Although the Tiddlingers were tennis aficionados, most felt that Otis was overdoing it. "When I was young, if you played tennis badly, you were considered a sissy in white pants," he was fond of saying. "And if you played well, you were considered a bum. Given the two alternatives, I understandably chose to become the latter, and I have devoted my life to it." He read nothing but tennis books and magazines, watched nothing but tennis matches on television, traveled only to tennis clinics or tennis tournaments, and neither smoked, drank, nor dated. His daily regimen began at seven o'clock when he arose, jogged in place for half an hour, breakfasted on wheat germ and ginseng tea, climbed into his Mercedes, and arrived at the club promptly at eight, just as Miss Agnes was opening the door. He would purchase a new can of balls from her, repair to the locker room to suit-up, and devote an hour to hitting his new balls against the backboard. "If you play with new balls," he would explain to anyone who asked, "you should practice with new balls. It's the weight factor that's crucial." Following his morning stint with the backboard, he would retire to the lounge and eagerly await the arrival of someone, anyone, who could be inveigled into a game. This was Otis's other social handicap in the Club. Because he would play with anyone, poorer players gained no points being seen playing with him. And while outsiders might laud his attitude as genuinely democratic, the true Tiddlingers uneasily looked upon it as leading, at best, to sheer anarchy.

The Professor, however, urged his students to listen to Otis play. "You will gain little by either playing with Mr. Otis or by watching Mr. Otis play," the Professor would note. "But, like most pursuits, tennis has a language of its own, a language you should master as quickly as possible to be accepted by the natives. The leading authority in this specialized linguistic field is unquestionably Mr. Otis."

It was certainly true that from the moment he stepped on the court and inquired, "Hot [cold, windy, foggy, etc.] enough for you?" Otis maintained a constant flow of cheerful chatter until the final point. If this point ended with his opponent's easily putting away a short lob, Otis would automatically ask: "Was that about the right height for you?"

Otis enjoyed lobs. For high ones, he would say: "That ought to bring rain." For long ones, he would advise: "Don't forget to touch all the bases." For those that he hit up into the sun to blind the enemy, he would offer the consoling remark: "You'll look good with tanned eyeballs." And when an opponent lobbed excessively, he would ask: "You play much ladies' doubles?"

A missed shot by the opposition brought out the best in Otis. "Five years ago you would have had it," he liked to say. He was also fond of saying: "Out late last night?"

"I'll take a little off my serve to get a rally going." "Ever thought of taking up bowling?" "How long have you had polio?" Or, if the ball would have obviously sailed out: "That's saving the fence."

In all fairness, he had, at last, an equal supply of comments for the points he lost. If aced by the server, he would respond with either: "Would you like to have that ball bronzed?" or, "Really, I couldn't have returned that one even if I *had* been ready." Otis would never dream of accusing an opponent of touching the net or of leaning over it to put away the ball. Instead, he was ready with: "Why is the net cord wiggling?" or his favorite: "Seeing my shot would've gone in the net, it's your point either way." When passed by the perfect shot, he never said anything other than: "Where were you really aiming?" And if struck by the ball anywhere near the groin area, he would titillate one and all by crying out in falsetto, "Nice shot!"

But the major portion of his vocabulary dealt, of course, with calls. Obvious service aces drew a comment of: "If you thought it was good, play it good"; "Ready when you are, C.B."; or, "That's me, always generous to a fault." Balls that landed within a whisker of the base line were greeted with: "Sorry, it hit the line and skidded out"; "Way, way out"; "Three-and-a-half feet out." Or he simply raised both hands to indicate this last measurement. Balls that landed three-and-a-half feet or more out elicited the advice: "Bring it in an inch and you'll have it." Otis positively relished close calls by his opponents. "The eyes go first," he would say. "Patronize your local optometrist." "I thought the lines were in." But he was equal to the occasion even when his shot struck the back fence on the fly. "How did you call that?" he would shout.

The other advantage gained by listening to Otis play was that, over the years, he had accumulated every conceivable reason for missing a shot. As the Professor pointed out to his pupils: "Should a player miss a shot for no good reason, he is not a good player. Therefore, to convince others that you are a good player, you must always have a good reason ready when you miss a shot. As you will miss a plethora of shots during any match, you will require a plethora of reasons."

Otis had them. They were based generally on visual, audible, natural, mechanical, and biological phenomena. Among the visual distractions were such sights as low-flying birds or aircraft which induced double faults, young ladies in brief halters, scraps of paper fluttering in the breeze, dogs on roofs, swooping kites, and any sudden movement by any person or any thing at any distance as long as he, she, or it was visible to the naked eye. Among the audible were police sirens, shouts of glee or horror from nearby courts, pages on the loudspeaker system, a cry of "whoops!" from an opponent who has hit a short lob, and the whine of power tools. "Wherever tennis is played in the world," Otis would comment on this last happenstance with a sigh, "you may rest assured that someone is either digging up the pavement or sawing wood." Natural visitations included the sun, the wind, and insects. The rays of the sun always shone in Otis's eyes when he missed an overhead—they were either beamed directly across the vastness of space solely for this purpose or cleverly bounced off a window pane, automobile hood, or lady's compact. Indoors or at night, as the result of modern technology, the sun's work was accomplished by the electric light. Thus the only time Otis felt ill at ease when winding up for an overhead was on cloudy days. The wind, suffice it to say, was always against Otis no matter which way it was blowing. Actually it blew only in two ways: it blew his shots out and his opponents's shots in. Insects were another matter. The small flying kind flew with incredible timing and accuracy into his eyes, ears, or nose as he was about to make an easy put-away. The threatening kind threatened as he tossed up the ball for his second serve on crucial points. And the crawling kind crawled across the court to interfere with his ground strokes. "I didn't want to step on him," Otis, the lover of all living things, would explain after flubbing a backhand as he gently picked up some poor, misguided beetle and carried it to the fence and safety. If it weren't an insect on the court, it was a rock. "That sure took a funny hop," Otis would say, stooping to search the surface for the offending boulder. Indeed, the Professor particularly admired this excuse, but he cautioned overly eager beginners never to employ it for missed volleys.

When it came to mechanical objects, Otis, like all tennis players, was more than willing to admit his mistakes. His mistakes included showing up on the court with the wrong racket, the wrong hat, the wrong pills, the wrong shoes, the wrong balls, or the wrong glasses. (He was careful never to mention this last mistake, however, if the subject under discussion were a close call.) Biologically, needless to say, Otis was the picture of Dorian Gray. In addition to the usual tennis ailments of interest primarily to orthopedists, acupuncturists, and elastic bandage salesmen, Otis suffered at one time or another from hangovers, acid indigestion, post-nasal drip, dropsy, double vision, three varieties of flu, including maybe even swine, dizzy spells, a shortage of wind caused by too much smoking, an excess of fat caused by giving up smoking in order to regain his wind, and a general debility caused by the starvation diet he had undertaken in order to shed the excess fat he had acquired in order to regain his wind. And, though he had never married, Otis had once proposed. His proposal was made on the spot to Elaine (Bunkie) Bigelow, who, after completely whiffing a forehand in a mixed doubles match, turned to him and said: "Ever since I had a face lift, my contact lenses slip."

Yet in victory, Otis was magnanimous: "I never saw you play better"; and in defeat, magnificent: "If I didn't let you win once in a while, you wouldn't play with me any more." Then he would take his leave with a wave of his hand and the inevitable: "Have a nice day."

But what had stimulated President Smeedle's sigh of resignation at the thought of selecting Otis to champion the Tiddlingers' cause was neither Otis's low social standing in the Club nor the prospect of having to listen to him play an important match. It was because—despite his dedication to the game—Otis had been shellacked every year for the past six years by the Crestmarshian's representative, Redford (Red) Head, a hard-hitting thirty-four-year-old attorney, and there was no reason to believe the results this year would be any different.

Actually, Otis was probably not the best singles player in the club. The more obvious choice was W. J. (Bull) Hammer. Mr. Hammer had enjoyed the top spot on the men's singles ladder for more than nine years, a feat the Tiddlingers attributed to his big serve, powerful ground strokes, smashing volleys, and to his not having been seen at the Club for more than nine years. This was, of course, the Professor's doing. The rules of the men's singles ladder were basically simple: "Any player may challenge any other player no more than two rungs above him on the ladder. The match will be played at a mutually acceptable time." This last rule was the key. As a star pupil of the Professor's, Mr. Hammer was extremely adroit at avoiding mutually acceptable times. "You say Monday at ten, Wednesday at five, or Saturday at eleven?" he would respond early on to some would-be challenger. "Let me check my calendar. Hmm. Damn, I've got an appointment with my podiatrist on Monday; Wednesday's out; and I'll be in Hawaii on Saturday. Why don't you give me a call next week, or maybe the week after? I'd love to play." After a few years, however, Mr. Hammer became jaded by all of this and simply secured an unlisted number. He is not forgotten, though, by the Professor. "Bull Hammer," as the Professor told Miss Merribuck, "is a credit to the Tiddling Tennis Theorem."

It was Doc Pritchgart who first suggested the Club hire a ringer. It's a wonder no Tiddlinger had thought of this before. Doc Pritchgart and Herb Smeedle were playing dominoes in the lounge on a rainy Thursday afternoon. "And six is fifteen for three," said Doc Pritchgart, laying down a tile and surreptitiously moving his peg forward four holes on the cribbage board which Tiddlingers employed to keep score. "What we ought to do is bring in a touring pro. He'd wipe those Crestmarshians off the court."

Smeedle reached over and shifted Doc's peg back a hole. "Oh, sorry," said Doc. "These old eyes aren't what they used to be."

"It wouldn't work," said Smeedle. "The rules of the Dee Cup state specifically that all players must be bona fide members of their respective clubs and must never have qualified for a major tournament—not that any of our members except Bang Banger ever have."

The Professor was seated on a barstool a few feet away, sipping his controversial lunch. On this particular occasion, the Professor removed the lemon twist from his mouth, downed the last of his martini, swiveled on his barstool, and surprised both Doc Pritchgart and Smeedle by saying, "I think I can help."

What initially surprised Doc Pritchgart and Smeedle was that the Professor spoke to them without having been spoken to first. But even more surprising was the Professor's unsolicited offer of assistance. (As Doc said later: "That was the first time in twenty years he ever volunteered to do anything.")

"You what?" the startled Smeedle asked.

"I think I can get you a ringer," the Professor said. "You'll have to make him a member, provide him with free food and beverages, and pay him a small stipend until the tournament. But I guarantee he'll win the singles, and you should thus retain the Dee Cup."

Doc Pritchgart idly moved his domino peg forward two holes. "I assume you've got some hotshot pro in mind, and you plan to disguise him somehow?"

"It's too risky," said Smeedle, shaking his head as he replaced Doc Pritchgart's peg in its proper position. "No matter how you disguise him, the Crestmarshians will spot a pro as soon as he starts playing."

"Oh, he's not a pro," said the Professor, examining his cigar. "As a matter of fact, he has never played tennis in his life."

THE TIDDLING TENNIS
CLUB RINGER

It isn't how you win or lose, it's whether.
—Roberts's Rules of Order

At nineteen, Beauregard (Bo) Jackson, stood seven-feet-two and weighed no more than 155 pounds. He had a small head, a short torso, and the rest of him was arms and legs, incredibly long arms and legs. The eldest of eight children, Jackson was articulate, intelligent, courageous, and a true leader of his companions. Unfortunately, his language, his problems, his challenges, and his companions were all of the black ghetto. Consequently, he had never done well in school. He considered academic English a subject as arcane as Etruscan vase painting, and by the third grade he had lost any interest in mastering it. Yet the teachers, to get rid of him, had kept passing him along. By the time he reached high school, he could write his name, forge the vice-principal's signature, and read such words as "Dick," "Jane," "Spot," and "Arresting Officer." But as a sophomore at Hudson High, Bo came into his own, for he possessed one attribute highly valued in the white man's world. "He's going to be," said his coach admiringly, "the best damn basketball player you ever saw."

Even as a sophomore, Bo towered over the other players. Moreover, he was both quick and well-coordinated. The photos his proud mother clipped from the sports pages at the time showed Bo leaping a good four feet into the air. In his sophomore year, he averaged a record thirty-four points a game and was already being taken to lunch by college coaches.

"Man, I don't know about this college shee-it," he'd say thoughtfully. "I got me too fucking much schooling already."

As it turned out, Bo's career was brought to an end at the beginning of his junior year with his third arrest for car theft. Despite considerable pressure from his coach and Hudson High alumni, a stern judge sentenced him to eighteen months at the Happy Valley Correctional Institution. There he received vocational training in woodworking, distilling alcohol from canned cherries, and the rudiments of safecracking. He did well in all subjects but woodworking.

By the time he was released from Happy Valley, Bo had reached the maximum age for compulsory education. And so he decided not to return to the groves of academe. "Man, there ain't no bread in it," he said in announcing his preference for a business career. Thus he devoted his evenings to practicing the vocations he had learned at Happy Valley, with the exception of woodworking, and

he spent most afternoons "messing around" with a basketball at the George Washington Carver Playground two
blocks from the Tiddling Tennis Club. It was there that
the Professor first spotted him.

The Professor had lived alone for years in an apartment
a half-mile from the Club in a respectable, if not posh,
neighborhood just west of the ghetto's boundaries. His
quarters consisted of one large room, a kitchen, and bath.
The furnishings were limited to roughly a thousand
books, most of them classics in philosophy and mathe-
matics, a hi-fi set and a record collection running heavily
to Bach, one easy chair, one kitchen table, one kitchen
chair, one Murphy bed that was seldom made and never
pushed back into the wall, and one desk cluttered with an
unfinished longhand manuscript modestly entitled, "The
Nature of Man, the Essence of God, and the Meaning of
Life."

It was the Professor's custom to walk home from the
Club each evening through the ghetto. As he had been
doing this for years, his Panama hat, cigar, and yellowed
flannels were a familiar sight to every ghetto resident. The
members admired his courage. Indeed, at one point, they
had hired a special policeman to escort them to their cars
in the evenings, but on the first night on the job he had
been mugged, and the agency refused to send another.
When asked directly by Miss Merribuck why he had
never been attacked on his stroll home, the Professor
simply replied, "No one gets mugged but strangers."

Bo Jackson's release from Happy Valley coincided with
the beginnings of the Tiddlingers' debate on who should
represent them in the Dee Cup challenge. It was thus that
the Professor passed by the fence around the George
Washington Carver Playground one crisp afternoon to
watch Jackson in action on the cracked asphalt basketball

court. The Professor knew and cared nothing about basketball. What intrigued him was not Jackson's superb ball handling and uncanny shooting, but a prank Jackson played on a shorter competitor. In the midst of the play, a grinning Jackson suddenly snatched the black leather cap from the other young man's head and, with a prodigious leap, deposited it not on the rim of the basket but on the top right-hand corner of the backboard. The Professor's eyes narrowed as he observed the subsequent pushing, shoving, and horseplay, and finally the persuasion of Jackson to leap up again to retrieve the cap, inaccessible as it was to any of the other players. Without a word, the Professor strode home at a quicker pace than usual, threw his Panama hat on his unmade bed, settled in his easy chair with the third volume of the *Encyclopaedia Britannica,* and leafed through the subjects therein to "Basketball." He next rummaged through his bookshelves until he found a pristine copy of the *Official Rules of the United States Lawn Tennis Association,* a work that had never interested him as no Tiddlinger had ever bothered to master any but the most rudimentary rules of the game. He perused several sections, nodding as he went. Finally, with a sigh of contentment, the Professor took out a pencil, a ruler, and a sheet of graph paper and began drawing diagrams.

The next afternoon, the Professor stood by the gate of the playground until the game broke up. As Jackson sauntered out, the Professor stopped him. "I have an offer, young man," he said, aiming his unlit cigar at Jackson's chest, which was at his eye level, "that you cannot refuse."

Jackson looked down on him suspiciously. "Haul ass, man," he growled. "I smell narc."

"He ain't no narc, Bo," said one of the smaller youths

who had gathered around. "He the Professor. He work in that honky tennis place. He okay, man."

A slow smile spread across Jackson's face. "You buying or selling, Prof?" he asked.

"Buying," said the Professor.

"What you want?"

"You," said the Professor.

Jackson grinned. "What you want me for?"

"I am going to make you," said the Professor calmly, "an unbeatable tennis player."

A slow chuckle began in Jackson's chest. It rumbled upward to his throat and finally exploded into laughter— lovely, musical, infectious laughter. The other young men caught it, and soon the whole group was convulsed with it, some doubled over, others slapping backs. Jackson poised himself on his toes, extended his right leg behind him, tossed up an imaginary tennis ball, and pretended to give it a genteel shove with the little finger of his right hand. "Tennis, man?" he said, when he had finally controlled himself. "That's for pansy honkies."

The Professor, who had been smiling quietly, nodded. "That is correct. And I assume it would give you a great deal of pleasure to defeat a succession of pansy honkies."

Jackson put a large hand on the Professor's shoulder. "I like you, man," he said. "But you jiving me? I mean, shee-it, I get my highs ripping off them go-go machines of theirs. Pleasure and bread. Man, you can't beat that."

"There is no reason you would have to give up your business pursuits," said the Professor. "All I would require is two hours of your time each afternoon. In return, I think I could offer you a membership in the Tiddling Tennis Club, all you could eat and drink in its restaurant and bar, plus, perhaps, a small weekly stipend."

"A what?"

"Some bread," said the Professor. "And let me remind you that the top tennis professionals earn in the neighborhood of a hundred thousand dollars a year."

"Hoo-boy!" said Jackson. "That sure do beat this neighborhood, man. You got yourself a deal."

"My only requirement," said the Professor, "is that you must at all times keep my teaching methods secret."

"Sure enough," said Jackson, still grinning. "Why for?"

The Professor smiled up at him and tapped his chest. "We will take the pansy honkies," he said, "by surprise."

7

THE TIDDLING TENNIS
CLUB DIRECTORS

*If you would become a master of the psychological pressure,
ploys, and convoluted machinations so necessary to destroy
your opponent on the tennis courts, become a director of your
tennis club. —Roberts's Rules of Order*

The number of directors of the Tiddling Tennis Club was
raised only recently from eleven to thirteen. The move
was made to make room on the board for Ms. Follicle,
whose persistent demands for sexual equality in estab-
lishing Club policy had grown increasingly irritating.
Indeed, she had gone so far as to take the unheard-of step
of nominating herself to the high post. In the past,
nominations to the board were made only by the nominating committee, composed of the same six directors. Each
year, the "Sinister Six," as Ms. Follicle loudly referred to
them, nominated themselves for another term and chose
five younger and, they hoped, docile members to assist

them in maintaining, as Doc Pritchgart invariably put it at the initial meeting of every new board, "the glorious traditions of our great Club." While the bylaws permitted nominations from the general membership, no member within memory had ever exercised this right. One reason, of course, was that the whereabouts of the only copy of the bylaws was a secret carefully kept by the Sinister Six. It was Ms. Follicle, naturally, who precipitated the bylaw crisis at the last general membership meeting, attended by the Sinister Six and twenty-eight general members.

"Point of order!" shouted Ms. Follicle, rising to her feet during a debate over whether to extend the Club's closing hour from ten to eleven o'clock each evening for the benefit of six domino players, five of whom were members of the Sinister Six. "I demand to see a copy of the bylaws."

"There is nothing in the bylaws," said Doc Pritchgart with dignity, "that requires the bylaws to be produced for any Tom, Dick, or Harry who wants to see the bylaws."

"I resent the male chauvinist implications of that remark," replied Ms. Follicle, folding her arms. "And how do we know there's nothing in the bylaws that we can't see the bylaws if we can't see the bylaws?"

"You can take my word for it," said Doc Pritchgart testily.

But the logic of Ms. Follicle's argument proved persuasive, and a motion to allow her to see the bylaws carried by a vote of twenty-seven to six with one abstention—that of Sean (Pancho) Scanlon, who had either fallen asleep in his favorite lounge chair or who had passed out. (No one could ever be sure about Pancho Scanlon.)

It was thus that Ms. Follicle discovered the provision in the bylaws, which were removed for the occasion from Herb Smeedle's safe-deposit box, allowing her to nominate herself. And that very evening, over dominoes, Doc Pritchgart persuaded the other four directors present to admit Ms. Follicle to the board "in order to prevent," as he said, "a divisive election battle, which would only stir up the members and which we would probably lose."

It was on the historic night of May 3 that the new board, comprised of eleven men, Ms. Follicle, and one girl, met for the first time. This last member was Margaret (Peggy) Conway, a large, soft, well-liked blonde in her thirties, whose timidity had recommended her to the Sinister Six. "I don't see where she can do much harm," Doc Pritchgart said over dominoes, where the political affairs of the Club were traditionally decided. "She's just one of the girls." But he had reckoned, of course, without Ms. Follicle, whose primary goal in life was to transmogrify every girl in the world into a woman, beginning with those in the Tiddling Tennis Club. She had taken to greeting Miss Conway by raising a clenched fist to shoulder level and, while the best Miss Conway had yet managed in return was an embarrassed smile, the two had been observed having lunch together in the Club lounge only the previous week. "It bodes ill," gloomily predicted the observer, Doc Pritchgart, with what turned out to be unprecedented accuracy.

So it was, then, that Herb Smeedle, whose turn to be President had not yet expired (the Sinister Six were scrupulously fair in rotating the presidency amongst themselves), took his place at the head of the table and delivered the traditional welcoming speech to the new directors seated on one side of the table, while the five old directors seated on the other dozed away. "And so," Smeedle concluded, "we can only hope that you new members of our hallowed board of directors will join with us more experienced members in preserving the glorious traditions of the Club. Now the first order of business . . ."

"Point of order!" said Ms. Follicle. "I want the record to show that I don't for one moment consider eleven men and two women to represent sexual equality."

"I'm glad you're for equality," said Doc Pritchgart. "That's the very first item on the agenda this evening."

"What agenda?" said Ms. Follicle. "Why don't I have a copy of the agenda?"

"We don't have copies of the agenda at our meetings," explained Doc Pritchgart. "We've found they restrict the friendly give-and-take so essential to preserving the glorious traditions of our great Club."

"Then how do we know what we're talking about?" persisted Ms. Follicle.

"We're talking about equality," said Doc Pritchgart.

"That's right," said President Smeedle, nodding. "The proposal before us—"

"What proposal?" said Ms. Follicle, her voice rising.

"I'm just about to explain it," said President Smeedle patiently. "The proposal before us is to provide a membership in the Club for a deserving Negro youth who lives across the street, in order to prove to our neighbors here in the ghetto that we are committed to the great American principle that all men are equal, no matter what their race, creed, or color."

"Or sex," said Ms. Follicle. "And what do you mean, 'all men'?"

"Well, he's definitely a male," said Doc Pritchgart. "And I feel we should put aside our petty differences in order to provide this fine young man with an opportunity to learn to play tennis, a game which instills a spirit of sportsmanship and fair play, and thus makes better human beings of us all."

"Well . . ." said Ms. Follicle.

"Good," said President Smeedle. "Then the motion's carried."

"Herb," said Doc Pritchgart, "perhaps you should mention the food and things in case it comes up later."

"Oh, yes," said Smeedle. "I should say the proposal we just adopted includes free lunches for this poor young man and a small payment of twenty dollars a week, so that he may help provide for his widowed mother."

This roused Gimper Mudge, the Sinister Six's crusty, penny-watching member, who had missed the last three domino games, and who was therefore unfamiliar with the ramifications of the proposal. "What?" he snapped.

"We have to think of it in terms of a scholarship, Gimper," said Doc Pritchgart. "You know, the kind they give deserving young athletes at college." He paused to emphasize his concluding words. "*In order to help the team win.*"

But Gimper Mudge was too outraged to grasp the hint, "Twenty dollars a week!" he said. "Do you think we're the Rockefeller Foundation?"

Smeedle and Pritchgart looked at each other. Pritchgart nodded. "I must ask each of you," said Smeedle, "to keep what I'm about to say in the strictest confidence, and I think you'll understand why. It so happens that this fine young man is a superb athlete. The Professor assures us that if we make him a member and meet his modest needs, he'll win the singles match against the Crest-marshians for us, and we'll retain the Dee Cup."

"You mean he's a red-hot tennis player?" said Mudge. "What's his name?"

"Beauregard Jackson," said Smeedle, glancing at a slip of paper.

"No Beauregard Jackson has ever won a junior tournament in the continental United States in the past decade," Mudge, who had an encyclopedic memory for tennis statistics, said suspiciously.

"Well, frankly," said Smeedle, "he's never played before. But the Professor has agreed to teach him."

"In three months?" asked Mudge incredulously. "It takes years to develop a good junior player."

"We don't know what the Professor has up his sleeve, Gimper," Doc Pritchgart said. "You know him, he won't say. But you can tell he's as pleased as a cat in a canary cage."

"You, of all people, would trust the Professor?" inquired Mudge.

"In a situation requiring secrecy, deviousness, and unscrupulous tactics," replied Doc Pritchgart with wholehearted sincerity, "absolutely."

"Well . . ."

"Good," said Smeedle, rapping his gavel. "Now the next order of business—"

"Just a minute! Point of order!" cried Ms. Follicle. "I want to change my vote."

"What vote?" said Smeedle.

"Well, I want to change whatever it was we did there. All this fine talk about helping a poor ghetto kid. And what you really care about is getting your hands on that obscene Dee Cup, which is a symbol of sexism if I ever saw one."

"Miss Follicle!" Doc Pritchgart looked at her sternly. "Do you mean to say you want to cast a vote against providing a poor but deserving young ghetto youth with the warm companionship the Club has to offer? Would you refuse to instill in him the spirit of good sportsmanship and fair play for which the Club is famous? Would you, in a word, deny him his inalienable right to an equal opportunity, his one chance to ascend the ladder of life and become a useful, productive member of our society? Would you, Miss Follicle?"

"Well . . ."

"Good," said Smeedle, once more rapping his gavel. "The motion's carried again."

"Thank you, Miss Follicle," said Pritchgart. "Let us never forget that this young man is just as good as the rest of us."

"At twenty dollars a week," said Gimper Mudge, "he's got to be a damn sight better."

DOUBLES AT THE
TIDDLING TENNIS CLUB

The secret of winning at doubles is to acquire, at all costs, the best possible partner. —Roberts's Rules of Order

With the singles and mixed doubles teams decided upon, it remained only to select the two outstanding athletes who would represent the Tiddling Tennis Club in the men's doubles match. There was little room for argument here. The names of Cranshaw and Pfeiffer led all the rest.

Though merely forty, Mellon F. (Mel) Cranshaw had developed a painful case of bursitis in his right shoulder that had forced him to relearn the game left-handed. This produced a painful case of bursitis in his left shoulder, the two cases being so severe he was unable to use an underarm deodorant. But by now he was ambidextrous and had therefore mastered an assortment of left-handed, right-handed, underhanded spin serves that bounced in an astounding variety of directions when they bounced at all. Because the ball bounced low, it offered little opportunity for a winning return among club players, particularly in doubles. Cranshaw never played singles. He was especially effective against strangers, owing to his method of warming up. He invariably warmed up right-handed, hitting moderately strong forehands and abysmally weak backhands. Once play commenced, his opponent, having sized up the situation, would naturally hit to where Cranshaw's backhand should have been. He would be greeted in return by the whistling left-handed forehand. This tended to distract Cranshaw's opponents as much as his underhanded serve, and it was generally not before the end of the second set that they finally became convinced he had no backhand at all.

His partner, Frederick (Fred) Pfeiffer, was one of the greatest practitioners of Brooklyn tennis the game has ever seen. Pfeiffer had the classic Brooklyn tennis strokes: (1) an adequate forehand, hit off the wrong foot; (2) a backhand that he employed only in the direst of emergencies and hit, when he was unable to run around it, on the wrong side of the racket; (3) a superb lob that invariably landed (in winds of up to gale force) from one to six inches inside the opponent's base line; and (4) a serve that startled adversaries by its total lack of either power or deception. Indeed, so soft was Pfeiffer's serve that it was claimed he could toss up the ball, push it forward, charge the net, crouch in the volleying position, and then look back over his shoulder to see if his serve was following him.

Nor was it true that Pfeiffer had never taken a conventional lesson in his life. He had taken one. He had taken it, oddly enough, from Whizzer Whitman, the Crestmarshians' classic tennis coach, who was not above instructing outsiders for ten dollars a half-hour.

"And what do you want to work on, Mr. Pfeiffer?" inquired Coach Whitman as he rolled his shopping cart filled with balls out to the net.

"Well, most people say there's something wrong with my backhand," admitted Pfeiffer.

"Let's have a look at it," said Whitman. "I'll toss you a ball, and you just swing away in your natural style."

"Where do you want me to hit it?" asked Pfeiffer.

"Oh, just hit it at me," said Whitman airily.

"Okay," said Pfeiffer with a shrug.

While Pfeiffer's backhand did happen to be upside-down, it lacked neither speed nor accuracy. Coach Whitman clutched his groin and crumpled to the pavement. It was a full minute before he was able to speak. His first words were, "My God, man, you're doing *everything* wrong."

Once the guilt-ridden Pfeiffer had helped Coach Whitman to his feet, the latter devoted a good five minutes to demonstrating the proper backhand grip, the proper turn of the body, the proper footwork, the proper backswing, and the proper follow through.

"Ready?" Coach asked at last, taking his position at the net. "Let's try it, then."

He tossed a ball to the intently concentrating Pfeiffer, who swung precisely as instructed. They both watched in silence as the ball soared over the fence and landed with a splash in the swimming pool.

"There," said the Coach with a nod of satisfaction. "That's much better."

It was Pfeiffer's last orthodox lesson. He took the others from the Professor, and he proved an apt pupil, for, like most devotees of Brooklyn tennis, he was a born winner.

First of all he returned an amazing percentage of shots—somehow or other—within the confines of the court. Second, his strategy was simplicity itself: should his opponents rush the net, he would lob over their heads; should they remain in the backcourt, he merely exchanged forehands with them until they, out of either frustration, impatience, or sheer boredom, went for a winner and committed an error. But most important of all was the psychology involved. Every opponent with classic strokes knew in his heart that he was far superior to the awkward-looking Pfeiffer. Every opponent was grimly determined to prove this point, not only to himself but to every other member of the Tiddling Tennis Club who might be watching. To prove this point, every opponent was required to hit incredible shots that would whistle past the indefatigable Pfeiffer. Unfortunately, most opponents were able to hit incredible shots once out of every three attempts, at best. Thus Pfeiffer consistently won two out of every three points. By the second set, his opponents were generally reduced to muttering, cursing, groaning, raging animals, and another triumph could be chalked up to Brooklyn tennis.

No one admired Pfeiffer more than the Professor. "Isn't it too bad," Miss Merribuck asked him one day as they watched Pfeiffer gradually destroying the sanity of two adversaries in a doubles' match on the court below, "that he doesn't have a decent serve and an adequate backhand? I mean he could be an excellent tennis player, couldn't he?"

"Sometimes," said the Professor, smiling contentedly, "I doubt you grasp even an inkling of the rudiments of the Tiddling Tennis Theorem."

"What are you up to, John?" she said suddenly.

"John?" said the Professor with surprise.

"I'm sorry," said Miss Merribuck, looking down at her coffee cup. "I thought by now we should be on a first-name basis, shouldn't we?"

"Of course, of course," said the Professor. He smiled ruefully. "To be perfectly frank, I had virtually forgotten it was my name. No one has called me 'John' since my mother died."

"Was she nice?"

"She was . . ." The Professor hesitated. "I suppose you might say she was a bit eccentric. I fear I might rightfully be accused of the same failing. Perhaps it's in the blood."

Miss Merribuck scratched her eyebrow with her fingertips, a gesture the Professor found somehow appealing. "Do you mean this Beauregard Jackson thing is just an eccentricity?" she asked.

"No," said the Professor. "Goodness, no." He stared out the window, silent for a moment. "Mr. Jackson represents the culmination. If my calculations are correct, this experiment with Mr. Jackson will constitute the proof I have long sought."

"Of your Tiddling Tennis Theorem?"

"Yes."

"How?"

The Professor shook his head. "If an experiment fails, the postulate on which it is based becomes irrelevant and not worth mentioning. But if it succeeds, Merri, I promise you will be the first to know."

Miss Merribuck smiled triumphantly. "Aha! You called me 'Merri,' didn't you?"

"I'll be damned," said the Professor.

In its initial stages, the experiment appeared to be working smoothly. On his entrance into the Club, Bo

Jackson had received a surprisingly warm welcome, both from Miss Agnes and the male membership. The primary reason that he and Miss Agnes hit it off was that blacks were not on her list of hates, there being but one Negro in the Club. Miss Agnes's list of hates, to which she added in her neat penmanship at least once weekly, began alphabetically with "All Members Who Forget to Put Their Charge Numbers on Their Chits" down through "Zoologists"—that being the occupation of a testy member who had had the temerity to complain that the laundry had starched his athletic supporter. Secretly, she felt somewhat inadequate, because she had never discovered anything to hate beginning with the letter X. But she was something of a favorite with the black children in the neighborhood, for when they rang the bell, she invariably rewarded them with a stern frown and an old tennis ball from the wastebasketful she kept by her desk for just this purpose. So when the Professor escorted Jackson through the door of the Tiddling Tennis Club for the first time, Miss Agnes automatically handed him a tennis ball.

"What for's that?" asked Jackson, squeezing it almost flat in his big powerful hand.

"No, no, Agnes," said the Professor. "Mr. Jackson here is a new member."

"Give me back the ball, then," demanded Miss Agnes.

With a grin, Jackson handed it over. "Members got no balls, huh?" he said.

"You can say that again," said Miss Agnes, and a smile, for the first time in the Professor's memory, flitted across her thin, wrinkled face. The clouds swiftly returned to her brow. "You will sign here, Mr. Jackson, and here," she said, pushing two forms at him. "And here is your locker key. Be sure to keep your locker locked at all times. These premises contain miscreants."

"They who?" inquired Jackson.

Miss Agnes nodded contentedly. "Thieves," she said.

"You can't trust no honkies," agreed Jackson.

"What?" asked Miss Agnes.

"He means white people," explained the Professor.

"You can say that again," said Miss Agnes and, to the Professor's surprise, she reached out and shook Jackson's hand. "Welcome to the Tiddling Tennis Club, Mr. Jackson," she said solemnly. "I feel strongly that we need more members like you." After he and the Professor left, she took out her hate list and stared thoughtfully at the H section.

The Professor led Jackson down the corridor to the men's locker room, which was the envy of every woman member who had ever seen it (usually following a Saturday Night Glittering Tennis Ball). Polished mahogany full-length lockers rose from the gold carpet to the ceiling with its soft, recessed, light panels. On the door of each locker was the framed photograph of its owner garbed in tennis togs, either standing by the net (if he was a poor player) or making what appeared to be an incredible shot (if he was good or lucky enough ever to have been photographed making what appeared to be an incredible shot). At one end of the locker room were banks of tiled, glass-doored showers with heavy chrome fixtures. At the other was the Viking Sauna with a neatly lettered sign on the door reading: "Members will refrain from drying clothing in the sauna at any time." Every ten feet along the walls was a mirror in a polished brass frame over a mahogany shelf loaded with combs in an antiseptic solution, bottles of hair oil, bay rum, and after-shave lotion, jars of Vaseline, and cans of powders and sprays for feet and armpits.

Jackson ducked under the doorway, looked around, and grinned. "Sure do beat Happy Valley," he said.

Herb Smeedle was standing in front of his open locker,

which, befitting the office of President, was located precisely halfway between the showers and the sauna, directly adjacent to a mirror. He was swaddling his portly midsection in a large club towel, tastefully imprinted with crossed rackets and the initials TTC. The Professor coughed to attract his attention. Smeedle turned, found himself staring at a frayed buttonhole on Jackson's chest, raised his eyes all the way up to the knitted maroon visor cap on Jackson's head, and gasped with startled alarm.

"This is our new member, Beauregard Jackson," said the Professor quickly. "And this is our Club President, Mr. Smeedle."

Smeedle dropped his towel, bent over, picked it up, and tentatively extended his hand. "Glad to meet you, Mr. Jackson," he said.

"Yeah," said Jackson, slapping his hand without much interest. "This stuff all for free?" he asked, picking up a bottle of bay rum and sniffing it.

"Certainly, certainly," said Smeedle, as Jackson removed his cap and began dousing his hair. "Help yourself. But, of course, you can't—ha, ha—take it home with you. I mean the bottle. I mean you can take home what you wear, of course. I mean, you know what I mean."

"And I get me one of these here lockers?" Jackson asked the Professor.

"Yes, I think Miss Agnes assigned you this one across from Mr. Smeedle," said the Professor.

"There's one available closer to the showers, if Mr. Jackson would prefer that," said Smeedle. "It belonged to Hiram Hotchkiss, God rest his soul. I don't think anyone's taken it yet. I mean, if Mr. Jackson would prefer it."

"This one do me just fine," said Jackson, cocking his head and looking down on Smeedle. "Do I get my picture on it?"

"Certainly," said Smeedle heartily. "Just bring one in, and Miss Agnes will have it framed for you."

"Well, now, I got me one from the front and one from the side. Which y'all think have the most class, man?"

"Whichever you'd prefer," said Smeedle. "It's up to each member to choose his own photograph."

"But remember to remove the numbers," said the Professor.

Jackson chuckled deep in his chest. "You mighty hip."

"Well, I think I'll get in that old sauna and sweat off a couple of pounds," said Smeedle, backing away. "Nice to have met you, Mr. Jackson. Welcome to the Tiddling Tennis Club."

"Right on," said Jackson. He turned to the Professor. "What for I need this here locker?"

"To keep your rackets and tennis clothes in," said the Professor.

"I ain't got none."

"I'll provide you with them. Two special rackets I'm making for you, shoes, two sets of whites—"

"I ain't wearing no honky-pansy little white pants," said Jackson firmly.

The Professor shrugged. "We will see. Anyway, keep your locker locked at all times. There have been some thefts lately."

"You mean 'fore I got here?" asked Jackson, surprised. "You mean you honkies rip each other off? My, my."

Just then, Smeedle waddled back, looking embarrassed. He shut his locker door and removed the keys he'd left in the lock. "Forgot my keys," he said, ducking his head. "Never know when you might need your keys."

"That's okay," said Jackson, nodding solemnly. "I don't trust these honky ofays neither."

The door of the sauna closed behind Smeedle. Thirty

seconds later it opened, and out came four members in various stages of perspiration with towels draped about their middles, beaming smiles plastered on their faces, and hands outstretched.

Ben Gantry, a mediocre B player, was the first to reach Jackson. "So you're the great Bo Jackson we've all heard about," he said, grabbing his hand. "I can't tell you how happy we all are that you've joined the Club."

"You is?" said Jackson suspiciously.

"Of course we are," said Gantry, still pumping Jackson's hand. "I can tell by one look at you that you're just what this Club needs."

Jackson nodded solemnly. "You, too," he said.

Other members emerged from the showers to swell the group around Jackson, each striving to shake his hand, size him up, and fawn over him as much as decency would allow. Jackson suffered as much of this as he could before finally calling loudly to the Professor over the heads of his new coterie, "Hey, Prof, ain't nobody in this place straight arrow?"

Needless to say, the warmth of the welcome afforded Jackson was not due to the racial tolerance of the membership, but to the fact that his arrival coincided with the annual mating ritual which preceded the men's doubles tournament. The news that the Professor was bringing in a secret ringer was certainly no secret, and the competition to sign up a genuine ringer for a partner was understandably fierce. The stratagems employed simply to sign up a modestly superior partner grew more devious with each passing year. In this respect, the Professor most admired the solution devised by Corwin (Horsetrader Al) Grodin, a stout, bushy-haired B player in his late forties. Three years before, Grodin had approached Gerald (Jocko) Simwyn, one of the most promising younger members of the Club, and hired him as sales manager of Horsetrader Al's Automobile Agency. The resultant drop in business was not so much due to young Simwyn's lack of knowledge and experience in that field as to Grodin's demand that he play tennis four times a week—always, of course, as Grodin's partner. Consequently, Grodin moved up from the B group to the A group overnight at an average loss of income of only $650 a month. But as he said to Mrs. Grodin, "It all goes to the damn government anyway."

Most members were not so fortunate as Grodin and were forced to rely solely on their wits in attracting superior players, knowing that precisely half their number were doomed to disappointment each year. During the weeks preceding the June tournament, the men's locker room, the lounge, and the courts were the scene of delicate hints, well-executed retreats, brash overtures, and hasty withdrawals that would elicit the envy of any amorous-minded whooping crane. This maneuvering was, of course, due to the Professor's maxim: *"Timing is the key to good tennis; therefore, never accept a slightly inferior partner until the last possible moment."*

Timing was of critical importance as well, the Professor emphasized, even in casually arranged matches. The maxim on his yellow card in this case reads: *"Always strive to be the third player to arrive on the court."*

"Arriving third means that the first two players are already on the court rallying," he explains patiently. "You can then decide which of the two is better, walk to his side of the court swinging your racket and say, 'Well, shall you and I take them on today?' This technique increases your odds of getting the best partner to two to one—the one being still in the locker room. Should all four of you arrive on the court at the same time, immediately position yourself with your back against the net post. This will enable you, once the first player walks on to the court, to roll either to his side of the net or the other side, depending upon his relative proficiency. Do not be the first player—under any circumstance. The man who saunters on to the court and says, as though it were a matter of no consequence, 'Well, who wants me today?' is treading on a psychological mine field.

"While securing the best possible partner is far more critical to the outcome than the actual play, perhaps a word should be said about the game of doubles itself. Once again, it is a question of timing—timing and teamwork. Where precise timing becomes essential is in communicating with your partner. For example, let us say he has hit a deep lob, sending one of your opponents scurrying back to the base line. You should, of course, compliment your partner with a loud cry of 'Nice shot!' With sufficient practice, you will be able to time your cry to coincide with the exact moment your opponent has completed his backswing and is about to attempt to hit the ball. Conversely, should you lob too short and one of your opponents is getting set to smash the ball for an easy put-away, you must warn your partner of the danger. You will find that shouting a properly timed 'Look out!' is generally quite effective, but be prepared to defend yourself at all times once the point is over.

"As to the value of close teamwork in doubles, I shall deal with that in my lesson on sportsmanship, which includes instruction in the delicate art of calling in-balls out."

_9_

TIDDLING TENNIS
CLUB SPORTSMANSHIP

*Always give your opponents an outrageously good call early in
the match to establish a reputation for fair play; consider this as
casting your bread upon the water. —Roberts's Rules of Order*

"Tennis," the Professor tells his pupil on one of his more
interesting advanced lessons, "is a game that traditionally
demands the highest level of sportsmanship from all
players. Take every advantage of this you can.

"For example, when you walk on the court to warm up,
take the side with the sun at your back. After hitting a
few, announce that you are ready to play whenever your
opponent is. He won't be any more ready than you are.
Generally, he will ask you to hit a few more. Glance at
your watch and tell him there certainly is no hurry. And
always remember the cardinal rule of rallying: never
return a ball that you have to move more than one foot to

reach. Merely let it go past and shake your head, thus impressing on your opponent the fact that he can't hit the ball where he wants to. Finally, he will announce he is ready. Never suggest spinning the racket to determine who will serve first. Instead, toss him the balls and say, 'Why don't you serve first? It doesn't really matter.' As you have had the foresight to place the sun at your back, he has the sun in his eyes. Traditionally, in non-tournament matches, the player with the sun at his back serves first. Thus, if he has an ounce of sportsmanship in his bones, he will toss back the balls, and you will not only have the advantage of serving first, but you will have established your reputation for fair play by having offered him that opportunity.

"Now then, let us turn our attention to the critical problem of calling your opponent's shots in or out. The card I have given you is lucidly clear about the necessity of making an outrageous call in your opponent's favor during, if possible, the first game. Try to pick a shot to call good that is at least four inches out. If he is such a good sport that he disputes your call, you know you have him. Simply say you clearly saw it good, and there's no room for argument. This not only enhances your aura of good sportsmanship but raises questions about your eyesight, which you can turn to your advantage in the later, crucial stages of the match. But what about the intermediate stages? Whenever possible, attempt to get your opponent to call his own shots. For example you are running for a ball that lands precisely on the line, and you miss it. 'Sorry,' you say, 'I couldn't see that at all. Was it in or out?' Your opponent, of course, saw it good, which it was. But should he say, 'It was good,' he is in the position of calling shots in his favor on your side of the net—a major violation of tennis ethics. As you have already established your good sportsmanship, he will be most reluctant to be outdone in such deportment. Therefore, the most he will generally say is, 'Well, I thought it was good, but let's play the point over.' The first time you have him in this position, you should reply, 'Oh, no, if you thought it was good, call it good,' and proceed quickly to the next point. He will now feel guilty and will henceforth hesitate to call his good shots good, insisting the point be replayed. The second, third, and fourth times this occurs, agree after considerable protest to replay the point. Following the fourth time the ball lands on or near the line, having firmly established your reputation for good sportsmanship and bad eyesight, simply call it out.

"In doubles, calling is far more complex. The best doubles' teams employ the good-guy–bad-guy technique, which police officers have found so valuable in interrogating suspects. In the early stages of the match, the good-guy member gives the outrageously good calls. It is the duty of his bad-guy partner to frown, shake his head, and say, 'Sorry, I thought it was out.' The good guy then responds, 'No, no, I was right on top of it and it caught the back of the line.' He then turns to the opponents and says, 'Your point, fellows.' Immediately, they look upon him as their friend in court, their knight in shining armor, defending them from the villainous perfidies of the bad guy. Later, when a ball lands on the line, the good guy should ask the bad guy, 'How did you see that, partner?' The bad guy's reply is, of course, 'Way out!' The good guy stares thoughtfully at a spot on the court for a moment before suggesting to his opponents, 'Why don't we play two?' By now the victims so loathe the bad guy and feel such warm kinship with the good guy that the good guy may take over the entire calling functions of his team, for no matter how outrageously he exploits his opponents' trust, the worst emotion he will arouse in their breasts is sympathy for his myopic vision.

"So much for calling. Now, the other occasion on which points are replayed is when a player, in the act of making a shot, is distracted by some happening not under control. A clear-cut case would be that of a player attacked by a large, wild animal while attempting to execute a top spin backhand. He would be entitled, and should be granted, the right to play a let. More common, perhaps, is a ball that rolls or bounces from another court onto yours during a point in progress. Technically, you are required to stop play if you wish later to claim a let, but tennis etiquette, if you play your cards right, will hopefully supersede mere technicalities. Thus, whenever you miss a shot, the very first thing you must do before throwing your racket is to look about for a ball from another court. Should you spy one, eye it balefully and shake your head. Your opponent, if you have him properly competing with you for the good-sportsmanship award, will inquire if the ball bothered you. Again, early in the match, you should reply, 'Absolutely not.' The second or third time, your response is, 'Well, I probably would have missed that shot anyway.' After that, of course, agree to replay the point even though the only stray ball you can find is up against the fence behind you.

"In doubles, your task is made easier by close teamwork. When your partner misses a shot and there is an extra ball lying around, inquire as loudly as possible, 'Did that ball bother you?' At the same time, be sure to point at the offending ball in the likely event it escaped your partner's notice. For if he replies, 'What ball?' the odds of your opponents' granting you a let are infinitesimal.

"Good sportsmanship also requires that you compliment your fellow players whenever possible. I have already mentioned crying out 'Great shot!' to your partner just as your opponent is attempting to return a deep lob. But one should compliment one's opponents as well. The time to cry 'Great shot!' to your opponent is when he has mis-hit the ball off the side of his racket for a dribbling winner. A better compliment, however, is invariably, 'Great get!' This is best said when your opponent has scrambled desperately across the court at the risk of a coronary occlusion to reach a superb shot of yours, which he manages to return feebly to you for an easy put-away. By crying 'Great get!' with all the admiration you can muster, you imply that it took a superhuman effort for a man in his condition even to get a racket on your superb shot and yet, despite his superhuman effort, he lost the point to you. This should instill in him a certain sense of futility. If he makes a superhuman effort and fails to reach the ball at all, the suitable compliment is a commiserating 'Nice try, old man.' If you are sure he is not going to reach the ball, turn away from the net and call out, 'Nice try, old man,' over your shoulder before he has completed his superhuman effort. This should take the starch out of him. We see, then, that 'nice try' is the most effective of all compliments. A word of caution, however. One should not employ it when an opponent double-faults for a fourth time in a row—not unless you are considerably bigger than he is.

"The principle of precise timing holds true as well when your opponent is serving. Should his first serve be three feet out, you should shout, 'Fault!' But beware of reacting too soon. In order to put him in the proper frame of mind, you should delay your shout until he is tossing up the ball for his second service. A word here about returning first services that are out. Should your opponent do this to you, you should make every effort to chase down his return and hit it back as though you thought your first serve was good. This demonstrates that he has thoroughly destroyed your rhythm and concentration by impolitely returning your out-serve and thus is required, under the rules of good sportsmanship, to say, 'Sorry, please take two.' If the circumstances are reversed, you must also say, 'Please take two.' But always add, '. . . if you'd like.' This encourages him to reject your offer or, if he accepts it, to feel guilty.

"Last, let us discuss the serve itself. The critical aspect of the serve in tennis is the position of the left foot. The rules of tennis require that both feet must remain behind the service line as you toss up the ball. Otherwise, you have committed a foot fault. Foot faults are only called, however, in major tournaments, when there is an umpire present in his chair. Thus the responsibility to avoid committing a foot fault rests solely on the server's spirit of good sportsmanship. I will merely note here that nine out of ten players footfault.

"Thank you. This ends our lesson in sportsmanship."

If the Professor's pupils ever failed to benefit from his wise teachings, it was not due to apathy, but rather to overenthusiasm. A case in point was Dr. Elford M. Bardworth, a leading gynecologist and mediocre B player. Following the Professor's lesson in sportsmanship, Dr. Bardworth began working on his serve. Within a matter of weeks, he had developed a technique that seemingly incorporated the Professor's theories to perfection. Beginning with the left foot planted across the service line, he would stride forward with his right, make his toss, take another step with his left, and smack the ball at his opponent. "That fellow Bardworth doesn't footfault," said Doc Pritchgart, observing him in action through the windows of the bar, "he yardfaults."

While Dr. Bardworth's innovative method decreased the distance between himself and the net and thus increased his percentage of successful serves, it created a growing resentment among his competitors. Partly, they felt that Dr. Bardworth was being unsporting, but primarily they were frustrated that they couldn't openly protest, because they all footfaulted themselves. The solution was devised by Paul B. (Peebee) Gardiner, a marriage counselor with a violent temper. During a doubles match against Dr. Bardworth, Mr. Gardiner's wrath grew every time the doctor served. Down one–four in the second set, Gardiner called out, in granite tones, "Service!" He then firmly walked fifteen steps up to the net, took the ball, and slammed it straight down into Dr. Bardworth's service court, so that it bounced far over his head.

"What was that?" asked the surprised Dr. Bardworth.

"That was my new serve," replied Mr. Gardiner grimly.

"But you can't do that," protested Dr. Bardworth.

"Why not?" inquired Mr. Gardiner sweetly, though his face was aflame.

The ensuing verbal altercation was the subject of delighted conversation around the Tiddling Tennis Club for a good week. As always, the members drew up sides. But in this case the verdict was unanimous against Dr. Bardworth, with the single exception of Mrs. Gardiner, who always was quick to leap to the offense against her former husband. Once Dr. Bardworth had been found guilty of bad sportsmanship, he slowly lapsed into Coventry. Superior players now avoided him at all costs. And while inferior players at first sought him out to improve their image, they soon found that, because superior players refused to play with him, their images were sullied rather than enhanced by being seen on the same court with him. Consequently, within a few weeks, Dr. Bardworth was reduced to hitting the ball against the backboard, which compares to tennis as masturbation does to copulation. After two desultory months, he disappeared from the Tiddling Tennis Club and, when last heard of, was reduced to playing volleyball two nights a week at the YMCA, a fate considered worse than death by any true Tiddlinger.

As an aftermath of the tragedy of Dr. Bardworth, the Professor was forced to print a second card for his lesson in sportsmanship: "*The critical aspect of the serve in tennis is the position of the left foot; it should be placed no less and no more than fourteen inches inside the service line.*"

TIDDLING TENNIS
CLUB HANDICAPS

The dream of every tennis player is to be burdened with the greatest handicap of all. —Roberts's Rules of Order

Doc Pritchgart's attitude toward the Tiddling Tennis Club's newest member, Bo Jackson, was somewhat surprising on the surface. In his youth, Doc Pritchgart had been one of the better A players, with a booming serve, whistling ground strokes, and a smashing overhead. But, as the years passed, his power gradually deserted him. Owing to his pride in his strength, he had never tried to develop drop shots, spins, and lobs, as had his contemporaries. Gradually, then, his game deteriorated. Inevitably, those who had long sought him out now avoided him. The fatal blow had struck nine years earlier. Doc Pritchgart checked the bulletin board for postings in an upcoming tournament and found the Professor had demoted him from the A flight to the B flight. Doc Pritchgart defaulted and two weeks later developed a heart condition, which forced him to renounce tennis in favor of dominoes, membership in the Sinister Six, and a consuming vendetta against the Professor and all his works.

The vendetta and its cause were well known about the Club. "I don't understand, John," Miss Merribuck said to the Professor over lunch one day. "You'd think he'd have been glad to play in the B flight, where he had a chance of winning, wouldn't you? I mean he wouldn't have had a prayer in the A flight, would he?"

"No," agreed the Professor. "But keep in mind that every tennis player not only thinks he is better than he is, but his primary goal is to convince all other tennis players to think so, too. He must worry not so much about winning an annual tournament but about arranging matches throughout the year. If he is placed in the B flight, he is an officially certified B player, and all A players are thus beyond his grasp. That is why I eliminated·the B flight entirely in the annual tournaments."

"You mean you have only one flight now?" asked Miss Merribuck, who paid little attention to such matters.

"Oh my, no," said the Professor. "We now have an A flight, composed of B players, and a championship flight, composed of A players."

"That's ingenious!"

"Yes, it's done much to soothe ruffled feelings," agreed the Professor. "And the inscriptions on the trophies are more highly valued by the respective winners."

Miss Merribuck laughed. "I think I see your fine Italian hand in the handicapping system for the mixed troubles tournament, too, don't I? I remember that last year Jocko Simwyn and I were playing with something called a 'minus-forty.' But Jocko seemed awfully pleased."

The Professor bowed his head modestly. "I must concede that it was a far more interesting problem. The directors, in their wisdom, decreed that every mixed doubles team should be handicapped in some fashion, so that all would be equal. Then they generously left it to me to devise the handicapping system. At first, I considered suggesting that all players carry added weights as do, I believe, racehorses. But the thought of asking Mrs. Boxlove if she would mind an extra ten pounds—when she weighs far more than I do as it is—seemed, at the very least, ungentlemanly."

Miss Merribuck giggled. "I love the thought of equating tennis players with horses, don't you?"

"I abandoned the concept as unwieldy and impractical," said the Professor. "I turned next to the more traditional handicapping system of bisques. That lasted one year."

"I thought a bisque was a soup."

"In tennis, a bisque is a point that a team can claim at any time during the match without actually playing it," explained the Professor. "For example, a team with six bisques, when the score reaches deuce, may exercise its right to claim two bisques, giving it the game, and still have four bisques remaining."

"That sounds charming. Didn't it work?"

The Professor frowned. "The problem was the positive nature of bisques. Only the scratch team was content. All the others, no matter how few bisques I gave them, complained that they were much too good to deserve that many, implying that I was obviously out to destroy their reputations as superb tennis players. They would then sally forth to the courts with their too many bisques and be slaughtered."

"Served them right, didn't it?"

"I saw that what was required was a negative handicapping system. I therefore now rate each team from minus forty to plus forty. A minus-forty team must win three points merely to reach love, while a plus-forty team needs but one point to win the game."

"What's so negative about that?"

"Knowing the nature of those with whom I was dealing, I was careful to give no team a plus handicap. I rated the very poorest at scratch, and they were quite content to be known as a scratch team. Even happier were those with minus-fifteen, minus-thirty and minus-forty handicaps."

Miss Merribuck clapped her hands. "John, you're a genius. But imagine people wanting a bigger handicap than they deserve. Aren't tennis players odd?"

"I'm not so sure," said the Professor gravely.

"What do you mean? . . . Oh, hi, Doc."

"Hello, Merri," said Doc Pritchgart, who was on his way from the domino table to the men's room. He nodded coldly at the Professor in passing.

"I can see now why he doesn't like you," said Miss Merribuck.

The Professor shrugged. "It's my fault," he said. "I should have eliminated the B flight earlier."

While Doc Pritchgart's attitude toward the Professor was easily explained, the warmth in his welcome of Bo Jackson was not. Doc Pritchgart, while not a member of NAACP, certainly didn't consider himself a racist. For example, he never used the word, "nigger," except when talking to someone he knew and trusted, like Herb Smeedle. Nor, though he drove a large Cadillac, was his car ever broken into when parked on the ghetto streets outside the Club. (True, he was always careful to leave a copy of *Ebony* face-up on the front seat.) As his tennis-playing days were over, he had no need to curry Jackson as a prospective doubles' partner. And the gangling Jackson with his knit cap and odd haberdashery, was certainly not "one of our kind of people," as Doc Pritchgart put it confidentially to Smeedle. Yet no one in the Club went further out of his way to make Jackson feel at home.

"I can't tell you how wonderful it is to welcome you into the Club," said Doc Pritchgart, pumping Jackson's hand when the Professor brought him up to the lounge to show him around. "Say! What about a nice steak sandwich? They make pretty good ones here."

"Don't mind if I do," said Jackson, eyeing Doc Pritchgart curiously.

"And a little wine to go with it? Sam's got a couple of bottles of a very nice Beaujolais tucked away somewhere."

"If it's red, man, I'll drink it."

"Good, good. Sam, a steak sandwich and a bottle of Beaujolais for Mr. Jackson here."

"A half-bottle," said the Professor. "He's in training."

"Well, what about two steak sandwiches then?" suggested Doc Pritchgart. "This boy looks a little thin, and we don't want our star players undernourished."

"Just one before his lesson," said the Professor. "We don't want him overexerting on a full stomach."

"Well, you can have the second one after your lesson, Mr. Jackson," said Doc Pritchgart, clapping Jackson tentatively on the shoulder. "We want you well-fed, content, and happy. And don't forget, everything's on the house."

Doc Pritchgart then retired to the domino tables with a pleased smile, and Jackson tore apart the large steak sandwich with knife and fork. "What's with that cat?" asked Jackson, his mouth full.

"I fear he lacks confidence in my ability to convert you into a virtually unbeatable tennis player in time for the match with the Crestmarshians," said the Professor, nibbling on his lemon peel. "If I fail, I will be in disgrace. The more complimentary food and beverages you consume, the greater my disgrace."

Jackson nodded. "You mean he's out to hang your ass."

"Well put," agreed the Professor.

When Jackson had demolished sandwich and Beaujolais, the Professor led him down to his small office behind the pro shop, unlocked the door, ushered him in, locked the door behind them, and presented him with a tennis racket. It was an ordinary-looking wooden racket, except that the handle was precisely fourteen and one-half inches longer than the standard model.

"Man," said Jackson, hefting it, "that's one long mother."

"So are you, Mr. Jackson," said the Professor. "So are you. Now let us discuss suitable tennis attire."

"I ain't wearing no pansy-honky white shorts, no way."

"You will be delighted to know that in the world of tennis, white is no longer exclusively beautiful. After a battle that lasted more than a decade, the last citadels of sartorial traditionalism have crumbled. Here at the Tiddling Tennis Club, after a spirited debate, lasting many months, the membership voted two forty-seven to one ninety-eight to allow players to wear any color and type of attire that was, and I quote, 'sold in tennis shops.' "

"That your hook?" asked Jackson.

"I do receive ten per cent of the proceeds from the pro shop," admitted the Professor.

"Well, now, I kind of like that. Hey, man, just give me a jock, and I will go turn them chicks on."

"I'm afraid the regulations also require you to wear a shirt at all times, not to mention shorts and whatnot."

"Shee-it."

"I have taken the liberty, however, of designing you a

special outfit that complies with the rules and should assuage your feelings."

"Yeah?"

The Professor unwrapped a package and withdrew an orange tennis shirt, size XL, and a pair of green shorts with a thirty-inch waist. "Orange and green, I believe, are the colors of Hudson High, whose basketball uniform you so proudly wore," he said.

Jackson viewed the outfit without much enthusiasm. "Too fuckin' flashy," he said, shaking his head.

"You might enjoy the embroidery," said the Professor. On the left breast of the shirt and on the cuff of the pants, where ordinarily an alligator, a penguin, or a fleur-de-lis was stitched, there appeared a small pig. And beneath that in discreet letters no more than a half-inch high was the legend, "Off the Mothers."

"Hey, man," said Jackson, "I do like that."

"You can thank Miss Agnes," said the Professor. "She is, I must say, a lady of delightful surprises."

With Bo Jackson properly equipped and mollified, the Professor embarked on his course of instruction on the teaching court in the farthest reaches of the Tiddling Tennis Club. The court's high fence, screened with green canvas, both insured privacy and titillated the curiosity of the Tiddlingers.

Actually, there had long been a move afoot, led by Doc Pritchgart, to take the teaching court away from the Professor and provide him with a corner of a storage room in which to give his lessons. "The last thing he needs to give those lectures of his is a net, white lines, and all that asphalt," said Doc Pritchgart. "And as for that fifteen minutes he spends tossing balls at his pupils, there's no reason he couldn't be replaced by a ball machine." While

Doc Pritchgart certainly had logic on his side, the traditionalists successfully argued that every respectable tennis club provided its professional with a teaching court, and said that the absence of one would reflect discredit on all Tiddlingers, young and old.

No one was more curious as to what was going on behind that secret-keeping fence than Herb Smeedle and Doc Pritchgart. Smeedle went so far as to play regularly on court nine, adjacent to the teaching court, in the hope of discovering some clue to the mystery. Even Doc Pritchgart agreed this was a supreme sacrifice on Smeedle's part. For, although Smeedle was only a B player, as President he was entitled to play on the much-coveted court one, where everyone could watch him make a fool of himself. Second, court nine was a grass court—that is, tufts of grass emerged here and there from the dirt—and Smeedle hated grass. "Just can't bend the old knees enough, and you know how low you've got to keep on grass, the way the ball skids," he told Doc Pritchgart ruefully. "I'm much faster on clay."

"The Club's eternally grateful to you," said Doc Pritchgart solemnly. "But what the hell is going on in the teaching court?"

"Damned if I know," said Smeedle, with the glum air of a master spy who has gone through untold tortures and returned without the microfilm. "All I know is that every once in a while you can hear a 'whop!' Somebody's hitting a ball real hard."

"Well, it couldn't be the Professor. I know in my bones he's never hit a ball in his life."

"I guess it's Jackson," Smeedle agreed. "But I'll tell you one funny thing: one time the ball came sailing over the fence and I heard the Professor say, 'Superb!'"

Doc Pritchgart was so stunned that he played his double five for twenty and moved his peg forward only a legitimate four holes. "You mean the Professor is teaching Jackson to hit the ball over the fence?"

"I don't know what I mean," said Smeedle moodily. "Who knows what goes on in that peculiar head of his?"

Doc Pritchgart smiled contentedly. "Well, all I know is that Jackson's run up a bar bill of forty-eight dollars and fifty cents his first week, and if all he can do is hit the ball over the fence against the Crestmarshians, the Professor is going to have to take up honest work."

Then, a rather odd thing happened. After two weeks of strenuously and mysteriously training Jackson for two hours every afternoon, the Professor abruptly terminated the instruction.

"You mean you've taught him all you know in two weeks?" Doc Pritchgart inquired politely.

"No," said the Professor. "But I have taught him all he needs to know."

The decision suited Jackson. He still dropped by the Club daily for a steak sandwich and a bottle of Beaujolais, for which he had acquired a taste, and he was still greeted warmly by male members who had not yet hooked a partner for the men's doubles tournament. He was, that is, until the Professor announced that Jackson would definitely not play in the event under any circumstances.

"It is absolutely imperative," the Professor told Herb Smeedle, who could be counted on to pass the word, "that Mr. Jackson's style of play remain a closely guarded secret until the Dee Cup match. If the secret is breached, the odds are precisely fifty-fifty that he will lose. If the secret is kept, the odds are at least ten-to-one that he will win."

"What the hell is his style of play?" asked Smeedle with annoyance.

"It is," said the Professor, "unorthodox."

LADIES' DAY AT THE
TIDDLING TENNIS CLUB

*Victory in ladies' doubles requires intense concentration on
every point that has previously been played.*
                                    —Roberts's Rules of Order

Ladies' day at the Tiddling Tennis Club extended from
nine to noon on Friday, these being the only three
hours of the week during which women had preference on the court. It had only recently been inaugurated
by the board of directors as a reluctant concession to Ms.
Follicle's demands for equal rights. Ms. Follicle, however, was far from placated. "Seeing that men have preference at all other hours," she said angrily, "I don't call that
equal one whit."

"I told you that broad would never be satisfied," Doc
Pritchgart muttered to Herb Smeedle.

But ladies' day, brief as it was, proved an instant

success for all but Melissa (Missie) Marshe, the afore-mentioned worst player in the Club, with whom no one wished to play. Had she been a sex object, she might have lured men into mixed doubles. But, while enthusiastic and ebullient, she was, unfortunately, chubby, bespecta-cled, and frowsy-haired. Her incurable inability to hit the ball within the confines of the white lines caused her to be shunned on the courts by her female companions. Yet she showed true grit. Every Friday morning, promptly at nine, Miss Marshe would bounce up the stairs and into the lounge, generally wearing a brand-new tennis dress, always carrying a brand-new can of balls, and displaying, at least once a month, a brand-new racket, which had "really made a tremendous improvement, honest." Miss Marshe was a cheerful, witty, good soul at heart, and the thirty or more women who had gathered to sip coffee, report on their children's triumphs, and discuss who was having an affair with whom, would greet her warmly and admire her newest tennis dress. Each Friday morning she felt as though she belonged. But as the level of the coffee descended in the cups, little groups of four would myster-iously form and chattily swirl away. By nine-thirty each Friday, Miss Marshe would find herself sitting alone, without quite understanding how this had happened. "I don't think I'll play after all today," she would say with a bright smile to Sam, the Club's beloved Chinese retainer, behind the bar. "Well, Miss Marshe, it is a little—" cold, hot, windy, damp (choose one), Sam would reply politely, his expression as inscrutable as always. Sam valued his inscrutability highly, since throughout his twenty-four years of loyal service to the Club his fantasies had involved how best to place ground glass in the peanuts, iodine in the Campari, and bamboo splinters in the vegetable salad.

Miss Marshe also decided every year at the last moment that she didn't think she would play after all in the ladies' doubles tournament. At least she got to play in the ladies' singles tournament, to which no true Tiddlinger paid much attention. She was invariably the first to sign up and the first to be eliminated, but this guaranteed her, in return for her annual dues of $300, two sets of tennis a year. Her determined cheeriness cracked only once. That was when Ms. Follicle, intending to be kind, assured her that she just knew her game would improve if she played more. Miss Marshe didn't say a word. She just stared wide-eyed at Ms. Follicle for a moment and then began to sob.

The ladies' doubles tournament followed immediately upon the heels of the men's doubles tournament. In the latter, to no one's surprise, Cranshaw and Pfeiffer won the championship division, composed of A players. The trophies in the A division, composed of B players, went to Feldon Greene and Gordon Cobb. Greene and Cobb were elated, not so much by the trophies as by the prospect that they would automatically be promoted the following year to the championship division, composed of A players, where they would unquestionably be slaughtered.

The men's doubles tournament was, of course, held on Saturday and Sunday. The following Monday morning, the ladies' doubles tournament began. As the women had to complete their matches by noon in order to clear the courts for the men (by order of the directors), the tournament lasted four days. It was won, for the fourth consecutive year, by the Twilling sisters, Madeline (Maddy) and Theresa (Tish). All but the Professor were confident they would be defeated in the finals this year by the formidable team of Karla (Bobo) Kampf, a broad-shouldered physical-education instructor, and Olga (Olga) Kanova, an equally broad-shouldered karate expert. Both were newcomers to the Club. Both were superbly confident as they strode out on the court in their shorts and shirts to face the Twilling sisters in their ruffled dresses. Their confidence turned to virtual contempt during the warm-up period, as they belted sizzling forehands and backhands at the seemingly-defenseless Twillings, who could do no more than block them back with delicate, ladylike, arching returns. Miss Kampf chose to serve first. Her serve was a boomer, and she charged to the net behind it like a water buffalo gone amok. "Oh, my!" said Maddy Twilling, holding out her racket. The ball rebounded off the strings, sailed a foot over Olga Kanova's outstretched racket and landed six inches within the base line. "Lucky!" Miss Kampf muttered as she retrieved the ball and prepared to blast one past Tish Twilling. "Oh, my!" said Tish Twilling, holding out her racket. The ball rebounded off the strings, sailed a foot over Olga Kanova's outstretched . . . The final score was six–two, six–love, in favor of the Twillings. The match was marred only in the middle of the second set by the angry comment of Miss Kampf, who, after netting her fourth consecutive overhead, hurled her racket into the fence and shouted at Maddy Twilling, "Can't either of you hit something besides a lob?"

"Well, we can," replied Maddy Twilling politely, "but we don't like to."

The Professor had naturally avoided being anywhere in the neighborhood during the course of the match. He had long since found that emotions rose during tournaments, that, if he could be found, he would be called upon to settle disputes, and that settling disputes between highly emotional combatants was unrewarding, if not downright dangerous. But he did stop by the bulletin board the next day to check the outcome. "Well, that was a surprise," he told Miss Merribuck at lunch. "How did those other two manage to get two games?"

"You're a great admirer of the Twilling sisters, aren't you?" asked Miss Merribuck.

"Certainly," said the Professor. "After all, the object of the game is to hit the ball over the net within the confines of the white lines. Ladies achieve this goal far more consistently than men, and the Twilling sisters are the most consistent of all."

"You don't mean women are better tennis players than men, do you?"

"Oh, far better. Compare the number of times the ball is hit over the net during an average point in ladies' doubles and men's doubles. Ladies are content with returning the ball safely, but men, to demonstrate their machismo, consistently go for a winner, which ends the point then and there, one way or another."

"But the average man can beat the average woman, can't he?"

"Oh, he'll score more points."

"Doesn't that make him better?"

"It depends," said the Professor, "on how you look at it."

Despite his avowed admiration for ladies' doubles, the Professor declined to give more than one lesson to any woman wishing to learn the fine points of the game, contending that all a player needed to know could be learned in a half-hour. The lesson began with the women playing a dozen or so points in silence. The Professor would then summon them to the net and inquire, "All right, ladies, what is the score?" The responses generally ranged from one–love and forty–love to love–one and love–forty.

"Fine," he would continue, pointing his cigar at a woman who had taken the former position. "Prove it."

"I just know it is," she would usually say with a petulant look. "That's all."

The Professor would shake his head. "That is not good enough for mastering the art of winning at ladies' doubles. To win, you must remember every single point played—every single point *that you won*. Don't worry about the others. Now then, let us attempt it again."

By the end of the half-hour, the Professor's students were generally capable of carrying out a suitably proficient ladies' doubles conversation:

"Well, that's game."

"No, I think it's deuce. Remember? You hit two backhand service returns into the net and missed that easy overhead when your bra strap broke."

"I know. That made it deuce. But then I hit that funny little shot off my handle, and then you double-faulted because you were giggling so hard over what Marge said about Bill and Esther, and you wanted to take two, but Marge is your partner after all, and we can't be responsible for what she says. So that makes it game."

At this the Professor nods approvingly and hands each of the pupils one of his small yellow cards: "*Victory in ladies' doubles goes not to the swift but to her who knows the score.*"

12

TIDDLING TENNIS
CLUB ETIQUETTE

Always carefully observe the rules of tennis etiquette so that you may best determine how to employ them to your advantage.
—Roberts's Rules of Order

July melted into August. All went swimmingly. "I'm thinking of having a sale of these," Miss Agnes told the Professor, thoughtfully holding up a heavy maroon jacket and pants with yellow stripes down the arms and legs.

"Warm-up suits?" inquired the Professor. "In August?"

"Sweat suits," said Miss Agnes, commencing to letter one of her signs. "Shed unwanted fat. I do believe a member could lose several pounds a set wearing one of these."

"Not to mention his grasp on life," agreed the Professor. "May Mr. Smeedle be your first customer."

"My," said Miss Agnes with surprise, "aren't we cheery! I suppose you think you've got the Dee Cup all wrapped up?"

The Professor shrugged. "Barring unforeseen circumstances, I should think we will win all three matches. But my only concern is the singles and my protégé, Mr. Jackson."

Miss Agnes nodded. "A nice young man. I think I actually hope he wins."

"You mean you would root for a member of this Club?"

Miss Agnes frowned. "Well, 'root' is a bit strong. I don't plan to be out there waving pompons, you know. Would you like a cup of tea? Damn. Wait a minute. I've got to run up the one–all flag."

From the vantage point of her office window, Miss Agnes could observe ten of the Tiddling Tennis Club's eleven courts, the exception being the Professor's teaching enclave. When all courts were in use, and members were waiting, it was Miss Agnes's duty to open the window and hoist a red-checkered flag to the top of a pole that rose above the clubhouse. This signified that players must complete the set they were engaged in as soon as possible and relinquish the court to those sitting on the sidelines. Under the unpublished traditions of the Club, the moment the flag was raised, the score on each of the ten courts, no matter how long the members had been playing, immediately reverted to one–all in the first set. Those waiting to play would then select the court that appeared to harbor the most one-sided match, on the theory that it would be over the soonest, and would sit on the handiest bench to help the players keep score. Even so, there were problems. No experienced member, for example, ever waited for a court on which Elmer (Skeet) Hoag was playing. Should Hoag get ahead five–one, he would begin experimenting with improbable shots. Inevitably the score would reach five–five, six–six, seven–seven . . . His greatest triumph was defeating Dr. K. E. (Kes) Wilson, a seventy-three-year-old gerontologist, thirty-two–thirty, while four increasingly angered members grumbled and fidgeted on the bench. This led to the directors' imposing a rule requiring a tie breaker when the score reached six–all. Unfortunately, the directors failed to specify which of the two types of tie breakers then in use should be employed: the sudden-death tie breaker, in which the first player to reach five points was declared the winner; or the sixteen-point professional tie breaker, in which the player had to win by two. Naturally, Hoag chose the latter, when the subject came up. And impartial observers were forced to admire the incredible skill he displayed in defeating Dr. Wilson, who he always defeated anyway, forty-two–forty, in what was undoubtedly a record tie breaker. The impartial observers did not include the four members waiting on the bench during this time. The directors were thus forced at their next monthly meeting to rule that the nine-point sudden-death tie breaker would prevail in all Club matches. Hoag, a deeply disappointed man, confided to his wife the next evening that a great deal of challenge had gone out of his life.

Naturally, the one–all flag did not apply to junior members. The Tiddling Tennis Club offered a well-rounded junior program for the children of members. Under the aegis of the Sinister Six, it consisted of a small, windowless junior room in the basement, furnished with four folding chairs and a discarded black-and-white television set, a sign at the entry to the lounge forbidding juniors to enter, and a rule permitting any senior member to kick any junior member off any court at any time. Complications arose when a junior member was playing a senior member. Fortunately, this was a rare occurrence. Senior members avoided junior members like the plague. "The trouble with these kids is that they lack court etiquette," complained Judson (Jud) Pourtney, "If they miss a shot, they stomp their feet and sulk around. It's really terribly disconcerting." While all senior members agreed, Pourtney's complaint might have carried more weight if he hadn't voiced it following his six–four, six–two defeat by fifteen-year-old Michael (Mickey) Kaplow. The match ended with Pourtney missing an easy overhead and setting what many believed was a new distance record for racket-throwing.

Seniors thus played with juniors only when they were blood relatives, or when they could find no one else available and were desperate for exercise. An abortive attempt to establish an annual junior tournament was made by Mrs. Robert (Millie) Prender, harried mother of five. "I feel we should encourage these wonderful young people to become more interested in tennis," she told the board of directors. "There's nothing like a tournament to stimulate excitement and instill in them a healthy spirit of competition, coupled with a respect for fair play and good sportsmanship."

"You're absolutely right, Millie," said Doc Pritchgart. "Where do you think they ought to hold it?"

This rather summed up the stand of the Sinister Six and other older members toward youth tennis. Or, as Herb Smeedle put it to Doc Pritchgart after that particular meeting: "Why the hell should we encourage kids to grow up to be tennis players? The courts are too crowded already."

But beneath this attitude lay still another factor. The Professor perhaps summed it up best on one of his little yellow cards: *Avoid at all costs playing with junior members; as they grow older year by year, so will you.*

13

TIDDLING TENNIS
CLUB CASUALTIES

Tennis is a game of concentration. You must therefore concentrate, first and foremost, on destroying that of your opponent.
—Roberts's Rules of Order

The Professor sat with Miss Merribuck in the Club lounge by a window looking down on court one, where the Thursday morning old man's game was in progress. The contestants were Judge Emmet (Judge) Fowler, seventy-six, wearing long white flannel trousers, which covered his knee brace, and a white blazer; Dr. Norman (Doctor) Fledgewith, seventy-four, wearing a white cap and elastic bandages on his thigh, both ankles, and forearm; Dr. S. Joshua (Doctor) Lewisohn, seventy-three, wearing a visor, a wrist brace, and elastic supports on both knees; and Mr. Hillman (the Kid) Reeves, sixty-nine, wearing a knee brace, a wrist brace, and elastic bandages on both ankles, both thighs, and both forearms. The contestants arrived in the locker room every Thursday morning promptly at eleven and were ready for action by noon, following exercising, bandaging, bracing, and hot compresses.

"It's wonderful, isn't it, the way tennis keeps people physically fit," Miss Merribuck said wryly, as she watched the players warm up.

"Miss Agnes thinks she can make a fortune," said the Professor, "by inventing a suit made of elastic bandages with zippers."

"You like her, don't you?"

"We've both been here a long time."

"And Sam. I don't understand him either."

"I wouldn't try."

"Does she understand you?"

"She who?"

"Miss Agnes."

"There's quite literally nothing to understand." The corner of the Professor's lips flickered in what was almost the beginning of a smile. "You see, I don't exist."

Miss Merribuck nodded at the martini in his hand. "You drink," she said, "therefore you am."

The Professor slowly took an old, thin black wallet from the hip pocket of his yellowed flannels, opened it, and removed a five-dollar bill, its only contents. "No identification," he said.

"Lots of people don't carry any identification."

"I don't *have* any identification."

"You have a driver's license, don't you?"

The Professor shook his head. "I never learned to drive. Neither do I have a social security card, a credit card, nor a bank account. My pupils pay me by check, and Miss Agnes converts these checks into cash, which I use to pay my rent and purchase my food. I have never been stopped by the police or fingerprinted. I have never taken out a passport, never having traveled, nor could I if I wished to, for I have no birth certificate."

"Was it burned in a fire?"

"No, my father was an anarchist-pacifist. He evaded the draft in World War I and never filed an income-tax return, not wishing to contribute in any way to what he considered the evil of government. During the twenties, he was a designer of peewee golf courses. Mother always said he felt it was an ideal occupation for an anarchist-pacifist. Unfortunately, he committed the disastrous error in 1931 of winning the Irish Sweepstakes. When reporters tracked him down, he told them he was as surprised as they, as he thought he had merely been contributing two dollars to a worthy charity. But the attendant publicity aroused the interest of the Treasury Department, and an investigation unearthed his long record of felonious high principles. A stern judge sentenced him to serve one-to-ten years. He said going to jail was one thing, but serving the government another. So he jumped bail and, as far as I know, the country. In any event, he hasn't been seen since. That was two months before I was born."

"But you were born," said Miss Merribuck, leaning forward. "That means you have a birth certificate, doesn't it?"

"I think my mother was always eccentric, but the disgrace turned her into a recluse. We lived in a big old house up on the hill then, a fine Victorian monstrosity. She gave birth to me in her bedroom with the help of her nurse-companion, and she adamantly refused to have the historic event recorded. 'There's absolutely nothing they can do to you,' she used to say 'if you don't exist.' And I never did."

"But what about school?" asked Miss Merribuck. "What about jobs?"

"She had me tutored at home. Luckily, we had the money. I doubt if poor people could afford not to exist. And this is the only job I ever had. I found the only two things that particularly interested me were philosophy and tennis. My mother didn't like me out of the house. But she always drank too much sherry at lunch; and when she slept in the afternoons, I would sneak out and come down here. It was the only activity in the neighborhood. The wall was merely four or five feet high then, with a wire fence on top. Anyone could wander in and out. So I wandered in and out, listening, watching. It wasn't long before I evolved my Tiddling Tennis Theorem. Actually, it was only a hypothesis then. But I compiled my little maxims over the years, and they became the buttresses of the final edifice."

Miss Merribuck laughed. "The what?"

But the Professor appeared absorbed in his story. "My mother died. I faced the problem of getting a job. I didn't want to apply for a social security card. I was afraid I couldn't get one without a birth certificate."

"I think you can, can't you?"

"I don't really know. But I preferred not to have one anyway. I would have had to write my name on an application. I've never written down my name, you know. And my name would have gone into a vast file somewhere. And once it entered that file, I would become known to them. I would be born. I would exist. I was too young for World War II. But there was a red-headed boy here then—named Danny Reilly. A good tennis player. I used to watch him through the fence, and he would smile at me. None of the other members ever did. I was always silent and solemn. I suppose they thought I was strange.

But they drafted Danny Reilly, and they sent him to Iwo Jima, and they killed him. And I realized then—I was thirteen or fourteen—that my mother was right: existing is hazardous to your health."

Miss Merribuck tentatively reached a hand toward the Professor's arm, paused, and then withdrew it.

"In any event," he continued, unnoticing, "what job was I fit for? I couldn't do anything, therefore I could only teach. The employment opportunities for philosophy professors without academic backgrounds were severely limited. Thus, this was my only alternative. And, I must say, I have been reasonably content. I haven't bothered them, and they haven't bothered me."

"I'm so sorry," said Miss Merribuck.

"Sorry?" The Professor looked up from his glass, into which he had been staring since beginning his monologue. "Good God, what got into me to tell you all this? It's almost as though by telling you—"

"Am I the only person you've ever told?"

The Professor waved a hand in dismissal of the question. "What matters is why. Why you?"

"Maybe it's because I hate singles. That means I'm either a very nice person or a very insecure one."

"And therefore not a threat?"

"Which do you think I am?"

"Frankly, I have never believed there was any difference."

"Maybe it's because I've had so much experience in being used," said Miss Merribuck, looking down at her hand. "My father used me to show off his money. He had scads. The best pony carts. The best boarding schools. The best of everything. My mother used me to relive her youth. How excited she would be when a boy asked me out. She would dress me herself and tell me exactly what to say and what to do. And she'd be waiting up when I came home to hear about every single minute of it. I remember once when I was eighteen I told her how a boy had made love to me in the back seat of his car. It wasn't true, actually. But it was the least I could do for my mother. She was in ecstasy for days. Then my husband used me to prove he wasn't a homosexual. Unfortunately, he flunked the test. You know, an experience like that is awfully hard on a woman. It makes her worry about her sexiness."

"It's a subject I know little about," said the Professor.

"Does she know you don't exist, too?" she asked.

"She who?"

"Miss Agnes."

By now, the Professor's voice had fully returned to its customary dry, crisp monotone. "I will say for Miss Agnes," he said slowly, "that in all the years I have been developing my Tiddling Tennis Theorem, she has been a constant inspiration in my work."

Miss Merribuck looked out the window and down on to court one, where the four old men were finishing the arduous chore of warming up. "I don't know what fascinates me about them," she said brightly. "It really isn't great tennis, is it?"

"To the contrary," said the Professor, "it's the greatest tennis played at the Club. Those four know every trick in the book."

"You mean trick shots?"

"No, no. I mean tricks to destroy the opponents' concentration. Watch closely. It always follows the same pattern. Dr. Lewisohn will serve first. He always takes four practice serves. All four will be softly hit with no spin in order to lull his opponent into a false sense of security. He does this only out of habit, as Judge Fowler, who is receiving, has been playing against him for more than forty years. Now then, Dr. Lewisohn is holding up the balls to signify he is ready to play. Watch. See? The Judge immediately holds up his hand and stoops over to tie his shoes. Well done, Judge! Now he's ready. The Doctor will serve into the net. There, he does. Now see how the Judge is crouched over, waiting with intense concentration for the second serve. Watch the Doctor. There he goes, tottering up to the net to measure its height with his racket. Obviously he could have done this before the match began, but whose concentration would that have destroyed?

"Now he will serve again. Look at the spin on that ball! But the Judge chops it back in a beautiful little drop shot the Doctor can't possibly get to. The Doctor will now say, 'Nice shot.' But his tone will convey unplumbed depths of sorrow and bitterness—sorrow that time has inexorably slowed his once-flashing limbs, so that he is no longer able to reach and easily put away a return such as that, and bitterness that any fellow human being would be so low and so base as to take advantage of the ravages of an opponent's advanced years. The idea, of course, is not only to create guilt feelings in the Judge's soul but to make him think twice before hitting his next shot. If he has to think twice, his concentration dissipates.

"The Doctor will now serve to the Kid. Aha! The Kid lobs one to the far corner. See how the Doctor staggers and stumbles to reach it. He can't. He clutches his chest. Then he shakes his head as though it were nothing. 'Nice shot,' he says again. The same sorrow, bitterness, and, he hopes, guilt. I think he has them now. Watch his partner, Dr. Fledgewith. He is superb, in moments like this. There he goes!"

"Where's he going?" asked Miss Merribuck.

"To retrieve the third ball that has rolled into the other court," said the Professor. "It's been there for ten minutes, but he wants to give the Judge and the Kid time to reflect on what they've done to his poor partner. Look how slowly he walks. It will take him a good minute and a half to reach the ball, pick it up, and return to his position. And during all that time, the opponents will have absolutely nothing to do but stand around and think. There's no better method of destroying concentration."

"Who will win?" asked Miss Merribuck.

"Oh, the two doctors," said the Professor. "For more than twenty years they've always won the first set six–four or six–three.

"But the Kid and the Judge seem to be in better condition. Don't they usually win the second set?"

"Who knows?" said the Professor. "They've never had time to play a second set."

14

THE TIDDLING TENNIS CLUB'S GLITTERING SATURDAY NIGHT TENNIS BALL

Given two athletes of equal ability, the one in better physical
condition will win. You should therefore attend your club's
social events to insure your opponent gets as drunk as you.
—Roberts's Rules of Order

The directors' meeting that August was memorable. Doc
Pritchgart opened with the happy announcement that the
athletic scholarship offered to Beauregard Jackson had
thus far cost the Club $278.92 in steak sandwiches and
Beaujolais. Herb Smeedle nodded and smiled. "He'd
better be good," he said.

Ms. Follicle, who was little interested in such matters,
raised her hand, her rigid arm indicating the eagerness
and anticipation of one embarking on a new cause.
Smeedle recognized her reluctantly. "What this Club

desperately needs," said Ms. Follicle firmly, "is the Roaring Snark."

"A roaring what?" inquired Smeedle.

"The Roaring Snark, for your information, Mr. Smeedle," said Ms. Follicle, "is a group of three fine young musicians, one of them female."

"They play tennis?" inquired Smeedle, who was still thinking of Jackson.

"No, they play music," said Ms. Follicle. "And they are just what this club desperately needs to attract more members to our Glittering Saturday Night Tennis Balls."

The Sinister Six sat in stunned silence. "Do you mean to say, Ms. Follicle," Doc Pritchgart finally managed to splutter, "that we should replace Bill & His Boys?"

Bill & His Boys (named Curly, who was bald, and Slim, who was fat) had been providing the music for the Club's social events for as long as anyone could remember. Bill played the piano with one hand, a muted trumpet with the other, or, if the piece so required, an accordion with both. Curly filled in on the saxophone, clarinet, ocarino, and kazoo, while Slim played the drums, always with brushes, the tambourines during the rendering of "Rio Rita," and the triangle for "Tip Toe Thru the Tulips with Me." It was said that all three had never changed their black leather bow ties, their white shirts, or their music in thirty years. They were highly admired by the Sinister Six, not only for superb musicianship, but for the fact that they played quietly, thus not interfering with the domino game that continued without interruption on Saturday nights in the far corner of the lounge.

"If I hear 'Harbor Lights' one more time," said Ms. Follicle, "I'll vomit."

"That tune always brings tears to my eyes," said Doc Pritchgart, shaking his head.

"You know, Doc," said Smeedle sadly, "it reminds me of the summer of thirty-eight at the old Avalon Ballroom in Catalina. I was—"

"The point is that the younger members want younger music," said Ms. Follicle, not to be dissuaded. "Last Saturday night there were only sixteen people here, and they didn't drink enough to pay for Bill, much less his Boys. We need a good, modern rock band like the Roaring Snark."

"You mean people drink more when they listen to rock music?" asked Smeedle.

"They have to," agreed Doc Pritchgart.

"I mean they'll draw more people, and the more people will drink more in the aggregate," said Ms. Follicle.

Smeedle sighed. "All right, I'll refer your interesting proposal to the entertainment committee. Who's chairman of that this year? You, Doc?"

"I don't know," said Doc. "I think so."

"Well, you are now," said Smeedle, banging his gavel. "Next—"

"Point of order!" cried Ms. Follicle. "It so happens that when you blatantly refused to appoint me to the membership committee, you instead appointed me chairperson of the entertainment committee, which, I was horrified to discover, hadn't met for four years. I therefore named Jim Stark and Peggy Conway as members of my committee. We met at my apartment last night, and it is our unanimous recommendation to the board that the Roaring Snark replace Bill & His Boys, who can, if they wish, go on to greater things at the Smithsonian. I so move."

"Second," said Stark, a young, dark-haired gentleman, looking at the ceiling.

"Third!" cried the once-docile Miss Conway, whose newfound boldness attested to the proselytizing abilities of Ms. Follicle.

The motion, as had become customary in this age of revolution at the Tiddling Tennis Club, carried by a vote of seven to the Sinister Six.

"The entertainment committee!" Doc Pritchgart muttered to Smeedle afterward. "Good God, why didn't you put her on the public-relations committee? It hasn't *ever* met."

The news that the Roaring Snark would play at the Glittering Saturday Night Tennis Ball created a stir in the Club. It was a most important ball. For while the Dee Cup match with the Crestmarshians was still a week away, the finals of the annual mixed troubles tournament were to be played the following day. It had been an exciting tournament thus far, producing three silent marriages and one permanent and two trial separations—not a record, by any means, but certainly enough fodder for an evening's gossip. The two teams that had survived and would play for the championship on the morrow were Bill and Janine Collums, of course, and, to everyone's surprise, Miss Candice (Candy) Kupp, a buxom airline stewardess, and Mr. Russell F. (Buck) Conrad, a criminal attorney. Miss Kupp was one of the worst players in the Club. Conrad was one of the best. Their success thus far in the tournament created numerous complaints. The Professor had handicapped them at minus-thirty. Those they had defeated complained that this team should have been handicapped at minus-forty, and the fact they had reached the finals proved it. But as this complaint was voiced annually, no matter who reached the finals, the Professor considered it inevitable and shrugged it off.

A second complaint, though not lodged officially, concerned the manner in which the attractive Miss Kupp had snagged Conrad as a partner. The complaints in this case were generally from married women in their thirties and forties. Their chief complaint concerned Miss Kupp's thin, tight, white T-shirt, which she wore without a bra in order to indicate to one and all that she was a liberated woman and certainly no sex object. The chief complainant was, understandably, Mrs. Conrad, a slender, sharp-featured woman. Mrs. Conrad's complaints began when the names of her husband and Miss Kupp appeared as partners on the tournament entry sheet.

"Well, she asked me point-blank," said Conrad defensively. "What could I say?"

" 'No'?" suggested Mrs. Conrad helpfully.

"I couldn't do that. Besides, I've always been interested in helping promising younger players."

"Promising what?"

"Really, dear, you know I'd rather have you as a partner. You could play rings around her."

"Then why didn't you ask me?"

"You know how these mixed doubles tournaments are, dear—the tensions, the quarrels. I guess it's just that I cherished our marriage too much to see it endangered."

"Hmm," said Mrs. Conrad.

Lastly, the few tennis purists in the Club complained about Conrad's and Miss Kupp's style of play. While Conrad appeared a bit nervous in the early rounds, he managed to pull the team through. His strategy was simplicity itself. Miss Kupp, who was able to return a shot to her forehand on occasion, was stationed in the right-hand alley with instructions to swing only at balls hit to her forehand side. Having deployed his troop, Conrad then positioned himself in the center of the court and played singles against the opposition. As his ability exceeded the average of his two opponents, he won. And Miss Kupp did, too.

So, in addition to the attraction offered by the Roaring

Snark, there would be a great deal to discuss at the Ball. By Friday, sixty-two persons had entered their reservations on the list posted on the bulletin board. What created still another stir was the entry scrawled near the bottom: "Bo Jackson and friends."

"Does an athletic scholarship include attendance at social events?" a scowling Doc Pritchgart asked Smeedle.

"I don't see how we can prevent it," said Smeedle.

"But what about these friends?" Pritchgart persisted.

"Think of all the liquor they'll drink," said Smeedle hopefully. "We always like guests at these affairs."

"At Club expense? Maybe you should talk to him about this."

"Maybe I should," said Smeedle vaguely.

That afternoon Smeedle waited until Jackson had finished his steak sandwich and most of his bottle of Beaujolais before making his move. Sidling up to the bar, he heaved his soft bulk up on the stool next to Jackson's and said to Sam, "Give me a vodka tonic, and put a little energy into squeezing the lime."

"Yes, sir, Mr. Smeedle," replied the beloved Chinese retainer, smiling his inscrutable smile as he dreamed of a jigger of Drain-O.

"Well, Mr. Jackson!" said Smeedle, as though suddenly identifying his seat mate.

"That's me," agreed Jackson.

"Herb Smeedle," said Smeedle, "in case you forgot."

"I did," agreed Jackson.

"Well, well," said Smeedle. There followed a few moments of silence. "I see that you're coming to the dance tomorrow night."

"That's so," agreed Jackson.

"Well, I just want to say how glad we are you can make

it. It's always good to see new members taking part in the social activities of the Club. I mean I just want you to know you are welcome."

Jackson sat up straight on his stool, took a swig from his bottle of Beaujolais, and looked down a foot or so at Smeedle. "That's mighty white of you, man," he said.

"Well, I just . . . Do you like to dance?"

"No way."

Smeedle looked relieved. "I guess you just like to listen to this new loud music."

"No way."

Smeedle frowned. "What is it, then, that you like about dances?"

"Jigging the chicks," said Jackson solemnly.

" 'Jigging'?"

Jackson leaned down to Smeedle's level, placed one of his long slender hands over the other and gave a fair imitation of a couple copulating. "Jigging," he said. "You dig jigging?"

"Oh," said Smeedle. There was another pause. "I see you're bringing a friend?" he asked hopefully.

"Friends," said Jackson.

"Oh," said Smeedle. "Well your friends are, of course, our friends."

"That's mighty white of you, man."

"But I was just wondering how many. The reason I ask is that we can only accommodate—"

"Two . . ." said Jackson.

"Oh, that's fine. Just fine. I'm sure they'll have—"

". . . dozen. Maybe three. But they dig this club shee-it. They got one, too."

"Oh, they're members of a club?" asked Smeedle, looking somewhat dazed. "Which one?"

Jackson drained his bottle, set it on the bar, stood up,

and looked down on Smeedle with a flashing grin. "Black Panthers," he said.

A few minutes later Smeedle bustled into Miss Agnes's office. "Where's the Professor?" he demanded.

Miss Agnes eyed him coolly, tapping a yellow pencil against her thin cheek. "He came in, examined the guest list for the Ball, told me he had suddenly developed pellagra, and went home."

"Why isn't he ever around when we need him?"

"Yes," agreed Miss Agnes. "He is good at that."

"Do you think I ought to call the police?"

"Pellagra's a crime?"

"No, I mean that protégé of his, Jackson. He says he's bringing two dozen Black Panthers tomorrow night. Maybe three."

"I doubt if I have that many tennis balls," said Miss Agnes with a frown, rummaging in the plastic wastebasket next to her desk.

"If he's inviting two dozen Black Panthers, I think I ought to invite two dozen policemen."

"I doubt if they'd get along very well," said Miss Agnes.

"I don't expect them to dance together," said Smeedle with dignity. "I expect them to watch each other."

"Yes," said Miss Agnes, nodding. "But I still doubt they'll get along very well."

"Oh," said Smeedle. "Oh, I see what you mean." His pudgy features contracted in concentration. He sighed. "Why do we presidents," he said wearily, "always have to make the agonizing decisions?"

In the end, Smeedle made the agonizing decision to do nothing. Word of what was up filtered through the Club. By noon of that Saturday, there were three apprehensive cancellations and forty-two new applications for reservations, which Miss Agnes firmly rejected on the grounds the deadline had passed. "What a shame," Betsy Cooper said to Lee-Lee Turgin between points on court four. "It sounds like this Club's first interesting social event in years.

To outward appearances, the Ball that night began as every other Ball had for years. Under Miss Agnes's supervision, the two old battered sawhorses were taken from the closet and set up in the lounge. Rested on these was a nicked and splintered sheet of plywood, the entire wobbly structure draped and concealed by a white table-cloth that had seen more pristine days. Miss Agnes saw to it that the stack of paper plates was placed over the wine spot that had resisted all attempts at eradication. The stainless steel bin of utensils and the paper-napkin dispenser were laid out. And, finally, Miss Agnes checked the kitchen to make sure the two large casseroles were in the oven, the two huge salad bowls in the refrigerator, the sliced bread in the baskets, and the pats of butter in their bowl of ice water.

"The salad supreme looks lovely tonight," she said to Sam, "if you like coleslaw."

"Yes," said the beloved Chinese retainer, smiling dreamily.

"Did they use pitted olives in the tamale pie?" asked Miss Agnes, eyeing the casseroles suspiciously. "That last one was a dentist's delight."

"Oh, yes," said Sam, smiling even more dreamily.

The preparations for another Tiddling Tennis Club Glittering Saturday Night Tennis Ball were complete.

As always, it was difficult to determine precisely when the Ball began. Around six o'clock a few of the middle-aged ladies who had been playing bridge and drinking slowly all afternoon, and a few of the older gentlemen who had been playing dominoes and drinking slowly all afternoon, put away their cards and tiles and scorepads so that Sam might spread tablecloths over the green felt-covered surfaces. They then, as always, straggled to the bar, stretching their muscles and chattering more volubly, and began drinking more quickly. By six-thirty, the first guests had arrived—Bill and Janine Collums. Collums nervously fiddled with his hearing aid and surveyed the room.

"I don't think she's here," said Mrs. Collums.

"Who's not here?" said Mr. Collums.

"Miss Candice Kupp," said Mrs. Collums. "I assume that's who you were looking for, considering you danced every dance with her last week."

"Actually, I was looking for Bo Jackson and his friends," said Collums with dignity. "As for Candy, she merely wanted some advice on her backhand."

"If it's her backhand that fascinates you, you're older than I think," said Mrs. Collums acidly. And as her husband's hand slid up toward his ear, she added sternly: "And, damn it, don't you dare turn me off!"

Other guests trickled in. By seven, the room was jammed, the tennis-playing members in their groups, the social members in theirs. It was not so much that the tennis members looked down on the social members, which they did, but that the tennis members usually talked of nothing but tennis, and the social members found it difficult to keep the conversational ball rolling. Tonight, however, the subject of all groups was Jackson.

"Do you really think he'll bring an army of Black Panthers?" Miss Kupp asked Collums, who just happened to corner her behind the potted rhododendron when Mrs. Collums had retired briefly to the ladies' locker room in order to adjust a visible brassiere strap her husband had kindly pointed out to her.

"Don't worry," said Collums in a deep, masculine tone. "We can take refuge in the sauna. Maybe we ought to head there now."

"Oh, I wouldn't miss the excitement for the world," said Miss Kupp.

"Nor would I," said Collums expectantly. "Let me buy you another martini."

At 7:48, Smeedle cried from the top of the stairs, "They're here!"

All the members turned toward him and stood like gulls in a pasture. Silence. Up the stairs came the Roaring Snark, two long-haired men and a long-haired woman (or vice versa, Doc Pritchgart later insisted). Each pulled a hand truck, to which was strapped a variety of musical instruments and electronic gear. The one with the beard looked at Smeedle. "Where do we plug in, man?" he said.

"Over there, I suppose," said Smeedle. "But you're forty-eight minutes late."

"You're lucky," said the one with the beard.

Around the room, shoulders sagged back to normal. The conversation and the alcohol flowed again. Sam carried out the salad supreme and the tamale pie, plunking them down on the banquet table. A few teetotalers lined up, paper plates in hand. It took a good twenty minutes for the Snark to untangle its nest of wires and plug itself in. "A-one," said the bearded young man, holding aloft his electric guitar, "a-two . . ." With "a-three," the fuse blew.

A babbling of jokes appropriate to the situation—such as: "Now you look much prettier"; "I knew I shouldn't have drunk that last one"; and "Let there be light!"—swept through the blackened room to be met by nervous laughter. At the head of the stairs, Smeedle, leader of men, lit a match. The little world it created consisted solely of a necklace of tiger claws gleaming against black skin, no more than a foot from his nose. Glancing up in awe, all he could see was a set of very big, very white human teeth bobbing in the darkness.

"Ai-yee!" said Smeedle quite loudly as the match went out.

"Ai-yee!" agreed Miss Kupp from across the room, for she had just been most painfully pinched.

"Ai-yee!" concurred Collums, whose wife had decided to cool his ardor with an ice cube down the neck.

"Ai-yee!" shouted Mrs. Hartford Hunt, who had lost heavily at bridge that afternoon and was therefore determined to win at some game before the day was through.

The room immediately echoed to the shrieks of women, the shouts of men, and the breaking of glassware.

Sam found the emergency flashlight in the emergency drawer behind the bar. The beloved Chinese retainer hefted it thoughtfully, heaved it across the room through one of the large plate-glass windows, and took a seat on the floor under the bar, clutching his knees and smiling inscrutably.

In her office downstairs, where she had repaired to man the buzzer for the barred door, Miss Agnes nodded complacently to herself, picked up the phone, and dialed the operator. "There is a riot at the Tiddling Tennis Club," she said calmly. "Kindly dispatch the police."

Captain Alan (Buzz) Sawyer, USMC (retired), a cool hand in any crisis, finally got his cigarette lighter working and, while shouting, "Keep calm, all hands!" made his way down a passage behind the bar to the fuse box. On his fourth try, he replaced the defective fuse. The lights blazed on, freezing the participants in an interesting tableau. In the corner by the head of the stairs, President Smeedle crouched under the coatrack, his eyes and nose barely visible between the folds of Mrs. Hartford Hunt's imitation ranch mink. In the opposite corner was the Snark, their bodies huddled protectively over their instruments. On the couch, passionately entwined, lay A. N. (Biff) Sawyer (no relation to Buzz) and Mrs. Babette (Babs) Treadwell (now the former Mrs. Treadwell). "We've got to stop meeting like this," she said moodily to her husband, George (now her ex-husband, George), as he peered down at her angrily. Along the far wall, one of the sawhorses supporting the banquet table had collapsed spread-eagle fashion. The salad supreme and a tamale pie had slid down to commingle on the floor in an unappetizing puddle that was already an inch deep. And in the center of the room, surveying with delight the world he had created, towered Bo Jackson, wearing a dashiki open to the waist, the afore-mentioned necklace of tiger claws, and blue tennis shoes.

"Man, when you throw a ball," he said to no one in particular, "you throw a ball!"

It was at that moment that the buzzer sounded below, and two policemen, one old, one young, came pounding up the stairs, white riot-helmets and plastic visors gleaming, handcuffs jangling, leathered holsters bobbing, and burnished nightsticks waving. The older one observed the scene at a glance through his squinting eyes, and thanks to a lifetime's experience in dealings with man's inhumanity to man, arrived at a quick decision. He nodded curtly. The younger one promptly grabbed Jackson by the back of his dashiki with one hand, pressed the nightstick against his throat with the other, and propelled him across the room.

"Feet apart, hands against the wall," said the young policeman.

"Why for?" said Jackson indignantly.

"None of your lip, boy," said the policeman, "or I'll throw the book at you."

"Shee-it," said Jackson. "This here's one hell of a way to treat a member of the Club."

"Who's in charge here?" asked the older policeman.

"I suppose I am," said Smeedle, untangling himself from the coats and brushing himself off. "I'm the President of the Club."

"Who started this riot?"

"Well, it wasn't really a riot," said Smeedle. "You see, the lights went off, and I'm afraid some of the ladies panicked. You know how ladies are."

"How'd that guy get in here" said the policeman pointing a thumb toward Jackson, who was in the process of being thoroughly frisked.

"Oh, he's a member of . . . You know, he's a member of the Club," said Smeedle. "He's on an athletic scholarship, of course."

"Of course," said the policeman.

Ms. Follicle pushed her way through. "Now will you let that poor man go?" she demanded. "I have never seen a more flagrant example of police brutality and racism. Furthermore—"

"We'll see, lady," said the older policeman. "We'll see."

The younger policeman had withdrawn a pack of cigarettes from a pocket of the cut-off Levis Jackson was wearing under his dashiki. Unfortunately, the cigarettes had never seen the interior of a machine. He handed them to his older colleague, who sniffed them and shook them out into his hand. "One, two, three, four, five, six," he said. "That's six counts of possession."

Ms. Follicle turned to Jackson. "You have the right to remain silent," she said, "and the right to the services of an attorney during all stages of the proceedings."

"Hey, lady," said the older policeman. "I'm supposed to tell him that."

"I was just making sure," said Ms. Follicle. "This poor young man needs help. The thought of putting him back in jail after he only recently won his freedom . . ."

"And one count of parole violation," said the older policeman.

"Don't help me no more," said Jackson to Ms. Follicle.

"Let's go, boy," said the older policeman.

"Don't worry, we're going to give you a great send-off," said Ms. Follicle. She aimed a finger at the bearded member of the Roaring Snark and waved it majestically. "Strike up the band!"

"Strike up the what?" said the bearded young man. "Oh, sure. What the hell. A-one, a-two . . ." And with "a-three," the fuse blew again.

This time, given the presence of armed officers and a desperate criminal in the darkness, the shrieks were instantaneous. Smeedle retired to his imitation-mink-lined sanctuary. The Snark embraced their instruments. On the couch, which they had never left, Biff Sawyer and Babs Treadwell resumed whatever it was they had been engaged in. And behind the bar, Sam, the beloved Chinese retainer, picked up a bottle of crème de menthe, the smell of which he had always detested, happily heaved it through the plate-glass window adjacent to the one already smashed, and returned to his fetal crouch, hugging his knees and smiling inscrutably.

"Keep calm, all hands!" cried Captain Sawyer, frantically spinning the wheel of his lighter.

In the office below, Miss Agnes sighed, picked up the phone, dialed, and said, "Operator, I think the Tiddling Tennis Club requires reinforcements."

When Captain Sawyer finally managed to bring light to the scene once more, the tableau was much as before—except for the addition of the two officers and the absence of Bo Jackson.

MIXED TROUBLES AT THE
TIDDLING TENNIS CLUB

Victory goes not to the swift but to the wily.
—Roberts's Rules of Order

Miss Agnes opened the Club as usual at eight-thirty the following morning. Sam, without being told, swept the shattered glass off court one and, while he was at it, retrieved the emergency flashlight, which was still intact. Among the first members to arrive were Smeedle and Doc Pritchgart, who sat in the lounge, drinking coffee and discussing the crisis.

"I guess we'll have to line up Oats Otis for the singles match," said Smeedle with little enthusiasm.

"I predict he'll be clobbered for the seventh straight year in a row," said Doc Pritchgart cheerfully.

"The darndest things make you happy."

"Look at it this way," said Doc Pritchgart. "The Professor's colored protégé is now on the lam. And he's left behind a bar bill of over three hundred dollars. Wouldn't it be a shame if it all went for naught?"

"Gimper Mudge would have the Professor's hide for sure," Smeedle said, smiling. The smile faded. "But what about the Dee Cup?"

"We'll win it with the doubles and the mixed doubles. I always thought that."

"Then why did you go along with the Professor on this Bo Jackson thing?"

Doc Pritchgart grinned. "For years I figured that if the Professor would just get himself involved in something, he'd blow it. And, sure enough, I was right."

Smeedle shook his head worriedly. "But are you positive we'll still win the Cup?"

Doc Pritchgart shrugged. "Who can beat Pfeiffer and Cranshaw? Who can beat the Collumses?"

The Collumses were on the court at 10:45 a.m., fifteen minutes early for their scheduled 10:00 a.m. mixed troubles finals match with Buck Conrad and Candy Kupp. The question of canceling the match because of the violence the night before was never brought up. It wasn't that anyone said, "The show must go on." To say such a thing would never have occurred to any tennis player. The Collumses checked over their equipment with easy confidence, their spat of the previous night apparently forgotten. It seemed obvious they viewed today's contest as simply a warm-up for next week's big game with the Crestmarshians. Mr. and Mrs. Conrad arrived together at 10:50.

"I always love watching Buck in action," Mrs. Conrad explained to the Professor, who, oddly enough, was waiting for them at the door.

"Whatever turns you on," said Conrad grumpily.

"May I see you for a moment?" the Professor asked him. "It's a matter of some urgency."

"But I have a match . . ." Conrad was obviously surprised to see the Professor making an overture.

"Yes, that is what I wished to discuss with you," said the Professor, "privately, if I may."

"I'll wait for you by the court," said Mrs. Conrad.

"You want me to lose the match with the Collumses so they'll be up for the Dee Cup next week?" asked Conrad suspiciously.

"To the contrary," said the Professor. "I sincerely hope you win."

"And you think we can? Nobody else does."

"Certainly you can. You have the attributes victory requires."

"Well, I suppose I am better than he is," conceded Conrad modestly. "But—"

"That, too. But I was referring to your partner, Miss Kupp."

"Candy? She has the strokes of a spastic."

"Strokes aren't everything." The Professor glanced over his shoulder. "Perhaps you would step into my office for a moment. I have an idea you might wish to consider."

Miss Kupp bounced breathlessly onto the court at 10:59, wearing briefer shorts and an even tighter, thinner T-shirt than usual. Across its back was printed the legend, "IT'S WHAT'S UP FRONT THAT COUNTS."

"Isn't that a commercial message?" asked Mrs. Collums.

"I don't know," said Miss Kupp. "But isn't it great?"

"They sure are," agreed Collums.

"May I see you a moment, Candy?" asked Conrad. "Privately?"

"Privately?" asked Mrs. Conrad.

"I want to discuss strategy with her," said Conrad.

"I think I'll go up to the lounge," said Mrs. Conrad, "and watch."

Conrad took Miss Kupp by the arm and led her to the far corner of the court. He talked. She nodded somberly. Once she giggled and only restored her self-control by holding her first three fingers to her lips. At the end of the lecture, she frowned sternly, raised a clenched fist, and said, "Got it, coach."

The Collumses had agreed on employing the Professor's confidence-destroying tactics for this match, as they felt Miss Kupp would have little enough as it was. So after they had warmed up for a few minutes, Mrs. Collums waited until Miss Kupp hit another shot off the handle of her racket and said sweetly, "We're ready whenever you are."

"Oh," said Miss Kupp. "Sure."

Conrad, who knew that ploy, quickly interjected, "Let me hit a few more at the net, please."

Naturally, after Conrad had hit a few more at the net, Collums was on him. "Have you had enough foreplay before we get down to the business at hand?" he asked with a smile.

"Foreplay?" Miss Kupp said with a titter. "Oh, that's funny."

"Yes," said Collums, "it reminds me of that old joke about the guy carrying this young lady into the bedroom, and she's saying, 'Foreplay! Foreplay!' and he's shouting, 'Later! Later!' "

"Oh, that's just hilarious," said Miss Kupp admiringly.

"Yes, that's sure a good one," said Conrad encouragingly.

"Shall we play?" said Mrs. Collums, frowning.

"You want to spin for serve?" asked Conrad.

"Oh, you go ahead and serve," said Collums, remembering his tactics just in time. "It doesn't really matter."

He reached up to turn off his hearing aid, but, just at that point, a smiling Miss Kupp mumbled something he couldn't hear. "What was that?" he asked eagerly.

"Oh, I just said you really have a marvelous sense of humor," murmured Miss Kupp.

"Well, I did write the Hi-Jinx Show in my senior year in college," Collums said modestly. "But I've never done much with it since."

"Oh, you should!" said Miss Kupp.

"Service?" inquired Conrad cheerfully from the baseline.

"*I* am ready," said Mrs. Collums.

"Sure, sure," said Collums.

"Okay," said Conrad. He then proceeded to ace Mrs. Collums with a boomer.

"Nice serve," she said without much enthusiasm.

It was Collums' turn to receive. He managed to get a racket on the ball, returning it weakly to Conrad. Conrad carefully lined it up in his sights and sent it hurtling at Mrs. Collums' head. Fortunately, she ducked just in time to avoid decapitation.

"Terribly sorry," said Conrad. "I was aiming down your alley."

"Nice shot," Mrs. Collums told Conrad grimly. And to her husband, who had forgotten somehow to turn off his hearing aid, she said, *sotto voce*, "You'd better get that little partner of his before he kills me."

Collums' opportunity for a defensive retaliatory strike

came on the next point. After several exchanges, Conrad lobbed short. Collums was in perfect position, just a few feet from the net. Just a few feet on the other side of the net was Miss Kupp, her racket held in front of her with outstretched arms and a happy smile on her face. Just as Collums took a mighty backswing, she bounced up and down on the balls of her feet as the tennis manuals instruct players to do while awaiting a shot. Collums swung. The ball landed behind him and bounced, bounced, bounced to the fence.

"Oh, what a shame," said Miss Kupp, cocking her head and arching her eyebrows consolingly.

"You might try keeping your eye on the ball," said Mrs. Collums acidly, "instead of whatever they were it was on."

"I forgot," said Collums.

"That's obvious," she said.

"No," said Collums, reaching up to his ear, "I forgot to turn you off."

Conrad won his serve at love. As they were passing at the net, Miss Kupp murmured something to Collums. "Beg your pardon?" he said, reaching up to switch on his hearing aid.

"Oh, I just wanted to thank you for the help you gave me with my backhand," she said. "Really, you should be a pro."

"Nonsense," said Collums, beaming. "It was nothing."

"I wish you'd watch my forehand. I know I'm doing something wrong. And if anyone can spot it, it's you."

"Glad to, glad to," said Collums obligingly.

"What was that all about?" asked Mrs. Collums when they had reached the far side of the court.

"Oh, she just wanted me to give some thought to her forehand."

"I'd prefer," said Mrs. Collums, "that you gave some thought to me."

"Your forehand is flawless, dear," said Collums sensing that a peace offering was in order. "And you've had a lot more experience than she has. I mean . . . That is to say . . . Damn, I forgot again." And once more he reached for his ear.

"Don't you dare turn me off," said Mrs. Collums.

Collums shrugged the shrug of an innocent man whose gallant intentions had been entirely misconstrued by a jealous harridan of a wife, and prepared to serve to Miss Kupp. Miss Kupp bobbed up and down enthusiastically. Collums double-faulted to her four straight times. The first three times he recouped by winning his serve to Conrad, once with a clean ace, and twice with spectacular shots that drew little cries of admiration from Miss Kupp. On the fourth occasion, however, Conrad selected a weak second serve and drilled it at Mrs. Collums' belly button, commencing his apology as the ball met his racket. Mrs. Collums, all akimbo, leaped backward to avoid the rocket, caught a heel, and sat down heavily, severely injuring her dignity.

". . . meant to go down your alley," said Conrad, finishing his profuse apology.

"Maybe I should wear a little arrow on my tummy which says, 'This way to alley,' " said Mrs. Collums with a glare.

Collums reached down to help her up. "What you should've done," he said, "is just hold your racket out in front of you. Let the ball bounce off it for an easy put-away. Nothing to it."

"I almost get killed, and you worry about the point?"

"Of course not. I just meant you're safer if you use your racket as a shield."

Mrs. Collums looked at the translucent strands of gut in

her racket and then at Collums. "I'd feel safer," she said, "if you tried that theory out on Miss Bazooms over there."

"I believe that's two–love," Conrad called from the far side of the court. "And it's Candy's serve."

"Kill," muttered Mrs. Collums.

But Collums seemed constitutionally unable to hit a hard ball at Miss Kupp. In fact, contrary to the entire strategy of mixed doubles, he rarely hit a ball to her at all. Instead, he smacked everything at Conrad, obviously relishing Miss Kupp's admiring remarks on the rare occasions when he got one by Conrad. Conrad, however, resolutely refused to enter into this machismo contest. Instead, he smacked everything at Mrs. Collums, who, in turn, attempted to smack everything at Miss Kupp, but she had little success, owing to the power of Conrad's shots. As Conrad was somewhat better than Mr. Collums and considerably better than Mrs. Collums, the contest deteriorated swiftly. Collums, usually the Rock of Gibraltar, began making errors. And under the immutable law governing mixed doubles, the more errors Mrs. Collums made, the angrier she became with her husband.

"Can't you hit the ball anywhere but to him?" she said, after flubbing an easy shot from Conrad.

"She's just a beginner," said Collums. "It wouldn't be sporting."

"Sporting? Jesus! And he's trying to kill me."

"Maybe if you played in the back court," suggested Collums helpfully. "Your net game seems a little off."

The helpful suggestion was as helpful as such helpful suggestions usually are. The next time Collums served to Conrad and charged the net, all colors flying, he was somewhat distracted to see his wife heading in the opposite direction at equal speed. Being distracted, he missed the volley.

"Where the hell were you going?" he inquired, being

no better with his hearing aid in operation than the next man.

"I was going to play in the back court where you told me to play," said Mrs. Collums with ill-disguised triumph.

"Not in the middle of a point, damn it."

"You know I just play worse if you criticize me," said Mrs. Collums and, quite naturally, she proceeded to prove her point.

With Mrs. Collums playing worse, the score quickly mounted. It was soon four–one in favor of Conrad and Miss Kupp. Now Collums began playing even worse. His problem was that everyone in the Club knew that his wife was a far better player than Miss Kupp. Thus if he and his wife lost badly to Miss Kupp and Conrad, everyone would believe Conrad was a far better player than he. His reputation, his male pride, his entire (to put it mildly) world were at stake. And there was his wife, petulantly blowing it. And there was Conrad, contemptuously and ungallantly blasting every ball at her. And there was Miss Kupp . . . Well, who could get mad at that cute, bouncy, smiling little thing? But he'd show his wife. He'd show the world. He'd show Conrad. "Kill the bastard!" he growled, tossing up the ball to serve to the black-hearted Conrad. Conrad returned the ball to a retreating Mrs. Collums. But Collums lunged in front of her, executed a magnificent dive which enabled him by some miracle to get his racket on the ball and send it weakly back to Conrad, who casually flicked it across the net to the side of the court Collums had deserted in his heroics. "Why didn't you switch?" angrily demanded Collums of his wife.

"I thought you were playing singles," she said.

Collums glared at her and prepared to serve to Miss

Kupp. Heretofore, he had served gently to her forehand. This time, she received a cannon ball where her backhand would have been if she a backhand. She gamely stuck out her racket, the ball ricocheted off the side of the frame, sailed thirty feet up, and arched gently down to where Mrs. Collums was standing at the net. Mrs. Collums turned sideways, swung her racket behind her shoulder, and pointed at the descending ball with her left hand— the perfect picture of an accomplished tennis player prepared for an easy put-away. Just as she was about to swing, a hand hit her shoulder, almost sending her sprawling. "Mine!" shouted Collums, and he sent the ball whistling at Conrad's head. Unfortunately, shoving someone out of the way with one hand while hitting a ball is a difficult feat demanding twice the concentration and dexterity as attempting either feat alone. Conrad ducked, and Collums' magnificent overhead smash hit the fence on the fly.

"Just out, old man," said Conrad cheerfully.

"Oh, that's too bad," said Miss Kupp sympathetically.

"Why the hell didn't you get out of my way?" said Collums accusingly. "I yelled, 'Mine!' "

"I thought it was community property," said Mrs. Collums, looking at Miss Kupp. "Or have you forgotten we're married?"

"There are times . . ." said Collums.

All that remained at that point was to get the match over with. Mrs. Collums, badly wounded, announced that she would follow Collums' instructions, as a good wife should, and both play in the back court and stay out of his way, thereby removing herself from the field of battle. She returned only to serve or receive serve, and appeared interested in neither activity. One thing that might be said for Collums: he didn't give up. Indeed, he charged about the court like a wounded water buffalo, making numerous improbable shots, each winning the acclaim of Miss Kupp and a dirty look from Mrs. Collums. Unfortunately, owing to the laws of probability, he missed more improbable shots than he made. The final score was six–one, six–love. They met at the net to shake hands. Mrs. Collums shook hands with Conrad and Miss Kupp. Miss Kupp shook hands with Conrad and Collums. "You played wonderfully," she told Collums, and that ended the handshaking, but Collums absent-mindedly held on to her. "You were just too good for us," he said, his customary good humor somewhat miraculously restored. The photograph, now in the Club archives, captured the trophy-award scene for posterity. Conrad and Collums each have an arm around Miss Kupp, who is holding the two first-place awards. A yard to one side is Mrs. Collums holding the runner-up trophies. All four are smiling—at least, Mrs. Collums' teeth are bared.

16

THE TIDDLING TENNIS CLUB
IN EXTREMIS

Just when you think defeat is inevitable, you are almost invariably right. —Robert's Rules of Order

It was Monday. The Professor and Miss Merribuck were lunching in the lounge (she was nibbling, he was sipping). The two shattered plate-glass windows had been boarded over, darkening the room and enhancing the gloom created by the disastrous events of the weekend.

"Is it true the Collumses withdrew from the Dee Cup match?" asked Miss Merribuck.

"So Mrs. Collums informed President Smeedle by telephone less than an hour ago," said the Professor.

"Just because Buck Conrad and that awful Candy Kupp beat them yesterday?"

"That may have been a factor, but Collums was also late to breakfast this morning."

"What's wrong with that?"

"As Mrs. Collums informed Smeedle with irate feminine candor, 'The son-of-a-bitch arrived through the front door!' "

"Oh. Who'll take their place?"

"Smeedle has already offered that honor to Conrad."

"Well, that's good, isn't it? I mean he and Candy beat the Collumses, so actually they're a stronger team."

"On paper. Unfortunately, Miss Kupp will not be Conrad's partner."

"Who says?"

"Mrs. Conrad."

"Oh. Well, she's a lot better player than Candy anyway. So they'll make an even stronger team, won't they?"

"True, except they will be operating under an overwhelming handicap."

"You mean? . . ."

The Professor nodded. "They're a married couple."

Miss Merribuck looked at him for a long, silent moment, but he didn't appear to notice. "What are you going to do?" she finally asked.

"I don't know," he said.

"It sounds now as if we'll lose the Dee Cup if Bo Jackson doesn't show up, doesn't it?"

"Probably."

"And if we lose the Cup, you'll lose your job, won't you?"

"Probably."

"And if you lose your job, all those yellow cards with your maxims on them . . . Really, your whole life's work goes down the drain, doesn't it?"

"True enough."

She scratched her eyebrow. "Do you know, I was reading them over the other night. I think I see a pattern in them."

"Very perceptive."

"They add up to something, don't they? I can't exactly put it in words, but I think I understand the feeling of it."

The Professor rubbed the twist of lemon peel once around the lip of the glass. "Do you find the feeling appalling?"

She nodded slowly. "A little," she said. "It means you've quit, doesn't it?"

The Professor smiled. "You forget. I never began. I'm an observer, not a participant."

"As an observer, you've managed to help muck things up a bit, haven't you?"

He shrugged. "I read the other day where one of the most difficult problems nuclear physicists face is to find methods of observing subatomic particles without affecting their behavior. The story evoked my sympathy."

"You really have to find Jackson," said Miss Merribuck resolutely.

The Professor smiled wanly down into his glass. "Oh, I think I know where to find him. But if I did, what would I do with him?"

"Well, you could tell him how your job depends on his playing on Saturday and—"

"Even if that plea moved him, which it might, he would be arrested before he completed the first set."

Miss Merribuck frowned. "But you can't just sit here. You have to have a plan."

"Oh, I have a plan. I always have a plan. This is a grand plan, and its deviousness and complexity are a joy to behold."

She leaned forward eagerly. "What is it?"

He shook his head. "Initially, I thought I might perhaps bring it off. And I must say, I accomplished its first phase with little difficulty. But the second phase would require me to become involved with affairs outside the

Club." He stared across the courts to the high stone walls that hid the ghetto beyond. "I never have, you know, and I'm a bit old to start in now."

"Damn it," said Miss Merribuck angrily, "you're already involved. You got Jackson into this. Thanks to you, they're going to catch up with him eventually and send him back to jail."

The Professor squeezed his eyes shut for a moment. "I know," he said. "I meant him no harm, though. He was simply to be the culmination of my Tiddling Tennis Theorem."

"I was always taught that I should return a tool or a book or a dress in the same condition it was in when I borrowed it. And whenever I don't, I feel guilty, don't you?"

"Yes, I know what you mean."

"So for both his sake and your sake, you're really going to have to get involved, whether you like it or not, aren't you?"

The Professor shook himself like a wet dog. The spasm quickly subsided. At the far end of the lounge, the movement caught Herb Smeedle's eye. "I think the Professor's sick," he told Doc Pritchgart.

"How come?" asked Pritchgart.

"He moved," said Smeedle.

"I hope it's nothing trivial," said Pritchgart, laying down a tile. "And twenty-five for five."

The Professor was silent a moment. "Perhaps you're right," he said slowly.

Miss Merribuck reached forward, and this time she put her hand gently on his arm. "You know I am, don't you?"

The Professor stared at her hand on his arm and then raised his eyes to look her fully in the face for the first time. He nodded.

"See?" she said happily. "You've begun already! I mean, you said you couldn't quit because you never began. That was the saddest thing I ever heard. But now you've begun."

The Professor smiled ruefully. "When can I quit?" he asked.

"When you're dead," said Miss Merribuck. "Now would you like to play tennis with me?"

"You must have ascertained by now," said the Professor, "that I've never played tennis in my life."

"Okay," said Miss Merribuck, grinning. "Would you rather go camping in the rain?"

"Good God!" said the Professor.

No one was more surprised than Miss Agnes when the Professor strode into her office and demanded to borrow a racket.

"A what?" said Miss Agnes.

"A tennis racket," said the Professor. "It is, I believe, an oval frame of wood or metal which supports interwoven filaments of gut or nylon, and to which is attached a long handle—the entire structure is designed to enable a human being to strike a white or yellow ball over a net, so that it lands between painted lines."

"Good for you," said Miss Agnes. "With your height and build, you'll probably want this Arthur Ashe Competition Two strung with French championship gut at about fifty-five pounds tension in a medium weight with a four-and -five-eighths-inch grip."

"Who's Arthur Ashe?" asked the Professor.

"Damned if I know," said Miss Agnes.

"And a can of balls."

"Personally," said Miss Agnes, "I'd recommend the

Australian-made Dunlops, not the American-made ones, which lose their numbers after a set or so on a hard court. Of course, if you're playing on grass or clay, the Wilson Championship, not the Wilson Heavy Duty . . . But then you won't be playing, will you?"

"As a matter of fact, yes," said the Professor firmly. "Miss Merribuck and I plan to hit the ball back and forth, and perhaps, with luck, even forth and back."

"Great balls of fire," said Miss Agnes. "What on earth will you think of next?"

All play on the courts stopped as Miss Merribuck and the Professor, racket in one hand, can of balls in the other, walked past, both looking straight ahead.

"Good God!" said Smeedle, viewing the scene through the last remaining plate-glass window in the lounge. "The Professor's got a racket."

"I've been saying that for years," replied Doc Pritchgart.

On reaching the teaching court, the Professor bowed Miss Merribuck in and carefully closed and latched the door behind them. For the next hour, the occasional sound of a ball being hit could be heard, interspersed with—and this is what the Tiddling Tennis Club members found most difficult to believe—laughter. As there were definitely two people laughing, and as there were definitely only Miss Merribuck and the Professor on the teaching court, the members reached the irrefutable conclusion that one of the laughers was the Professor.

"Impossible," said Smeedle on being informed of the phenomenon by his wife, Bootsy. "He doesn't know how."

"The Dee Cup's as good as lost, and he's laughing?" said Doc Pritchgart. "Too bad he didn't live in Pompeii. He would have found the eruption hilarious."

After the hour's session, Miss Merribuck emerged as cool and crisp as ever. The Professor was perspiring profusely, a sight as unique as the sound of his laughter.

"Did you really enjoy it?" Miss Merribuck asked, as they settled down in the lounge for lunch.

"I'm shocked to say that I did," said the Professor, smiling at her, "though it violated all the principles I hold most dear. You are bound and determined to get me involved, aren't you?"

"Yes," said Miss Merribuck.

"But what of the game I invented? Did it bore you? I'm afraid I'm not much good at winning."

Miss Merribuck grinned at him. "My husband was a winner. The trouble with being married to a winner," she said, "is that you have to be a loser."

Smeedle stopped by their table. "How are the lessons going," he asked.

"Fine," said Miss Merribuck.

"Are you learning much?"

"He's a marvelous teacher, isn't he?"

"What are you working on?" persisted Smeedle.

"Cooperative tennis," said Miss Merribuck, taking a dainty bite of her fruit compote. "We had our very first match today."

"Who won?"

"We did."

"Who did?"

"We both did. You see, in cooperative tennis the idea is to hit the ball over the net within the lines as many times as possible. When one of us hits it over, it's a victory for both of us. When one of us fails, it's a defeat for both of us. But we succeeded far more often than we failed, so both of us won, don't you see?"

"Sounds dull," said Smeedle and he turned to the

Professor. "More to the point, what are you doing about the Dee Cup?"

"I have a plan," said the Professor gravely, "a secret plan."

"Do you think it'll work?"

The Professor shrugged. "Time will tell," he said, and that was all he would say for the remainder of the week.

"He always was a mysterious bastard," said Doc Pritchgart.

"I don't think he has a plan at all," said Smeedle.

Doc Pritchgart shook his head. "If there's one thing you can have faith in during the upsetting times we live in," he said somberly, "it's the Professor's monumental deviousness."

On Friday afternoon, Beauregard Jackson was arrested while shooting baskets at the George Washington Carver Playground "on," as the arresting officer noted in his report, "information received."

17

THE TIDDLING TENNIS CLUB
STRUGGLES BACK

The sole problem with hitting an impossible shot is that it is impossible. —Roberts's Rules of Order

The day of the Dee Cup Match between the Crestmarsh Racquet Club and the Tiddling Tennis Club dawned, as God willed, bright and clear. The first match, men's doubles, was scheduled for ten o'clock, meaning it would begin precisely at eleven o'clock. The Crestmarshians arrived in force from suburbia, fifty-strong. They were distinguished from the Tiddlingers by the fact that they arrived at ten instead of eleven and by the color of their skins. The females, oriented toward swimming pools and halter tops, were more tanned; the males, who spent an hour or two a day cooped up in cars, buses, or trains so that they might enjoy their pastoral, sunny patios if they arrived home before dark, were more pale.

The Professor himself arrived at ten-thirty. "I thought I would get here early to be sure everything was properly prepared," he told a surprised Miss Agnes.

What surprised Miss Agnes was that the Professor showed up at all, for he usually avoided tournaments, especially the one for the Dee Cup.

"Whatever's gotten into you?" she asked.

The Professor looked at her and smiled.

"Well," conceded Miss Agnes, tapping her yellow pencil against her chin, "she's the best of the lot."

"Do you really think so?" asked the Professor happily. And he bustled off.

The old temporary grandstands, with their four rows of splintered wooden seats, which were dragged out of storage only once or twice a year, had been erected on court two, facing court one. The Crestmarshians gathered in a gaggle at one end, spreading out blankets, opening Thermos bottles, some of which contained coffee, and eyeing with cool disdain the few Tiddlingers who had shown up on the premises at that ungodly hour. Their men's doubles champions were already out on the court, warming up against each other. One was Peter (Dick) Richards, twenty, who was eligible for the Dee Cup on the grounds he had never qualified for a major tournament—the primary reason being he had never deigned to enter one. He was a dark, handsome, cocky young man in spotless whites, who hit his ground strokes and volleys with effortless ease, occasionally returning a ball from between his legs or from behind his back. His partner was Elmer (Bubba) Byznewski, six feet two, 220 pounds, and one of professional football's all-time great linebackers. Byznewski had taken up tennis only recently, at the age of forty-two. He brought to the sport a right knee that bent equally well in any direction unless heavily braced and bandaged, pins in both shoulders, a

glowering scar bisecting his bushy left eyebrow, a flashing smile of predominantly artificial teeth, and, like all
former professional football players, an indomitable will
to win. Almost everyone agreed that he was a most
pleasant competitor because he was always smiling.
When ahead five–love and forty–love, Byznewski would
turn to his partner with his pleasing grin and say softly
through clenched teeth, "Kill the bastards." He grasped
the racket like a club, although in his huge hands it took
on more the aspect of a Ping-pong paddle. He had a
pushy little serve which he would follow lumberingly to
the net. He would stand there and wait, baring his teeth,
like a caged lion at feeding time. When the ball arrived
anywhere in his vicinity, he never hit it. He swatted it as
one would swat a fly. That ended the point.

Up in the lounge, the Professor paused before the
newly replaced plate-glass windows to observe the Crestmarshian men's doubles team. He was joined by Miss
Merribuck, who was wearing a crisp white tennis dress,
her black hair pulled behind her head in a white ribbon.
She looked at him anxiously. "Is everything all right?"
she asked.

"Thus far," said the Professor, "all the components are
proceeding according to schedule. It is essential, however, that we win this men's doubles match."

Miss Merribuck looked down to watch young Dick
Richards' fluid strokes and easy grace. "I don't know,"
she said, sounding worried, "he looks awfully good,
doesn't he?"

"Very effective," agreed the Professor. "I trust Cranshaw and Pfeiffer will realize this and devise a winning
strategy."

"Are you sure he isn't a ringer? He looks good enough
to be a professional, doesn't he?"

"I understand he was for ten or fifteen years—a professional football player, that is. They're the worst kind."

"But he doesn't look like . . . Oh, I'm sorry. I was talking about the younger one."

The Professor glanced at Richards, as though for the first time. "Him?" he said. "Oh, he's no threat."

The Professor's analysis proved uncannily accurate. By 10:45, the Tiddlingers began arriving, and at precisely 10:59, sixty seconds before the default deadline, Mellon F. Cranshaw and Fred Pfeiffer took the court to a smattering of wry applause. After handshakes and the requisite apologies for being late ("You know, we forgot completely we had this match today"), Cranshaw spun his racket. "Up or down?" he inquired, referring to the trade-mark on the butt of the handle. The Crestmarshians won the spin and elected to serve first, as tournament players almost inevitably do. They were somewhat surprised when the Tiddlingers chose to receive on the shady side. This was, of course, a strategem taught by the Professor. "First of all," he would lecture, "most players who lose the spin elect to receive with the sun in their eyes so that, following the change of courts after the first game, they can serve with the sun at their backs. Thus by violating this tradition, your opponents will wonder what you are up to. Second, your opponents will have planned to put their strongest server up first. He will have to serve with the sun in his eyes. Being the stronger server, he is, of course, accustomed to serving with the sun at his back. This, then, should annoy him to no end."

After a brief warm-up ("That's all we need," Cranshaw called across the net), Richards, frowning and squinting into the sun, prepared to serve. His serve was a boomer, totally without guile. Cranshaw and Pfeiffer had little difficulty in blocking it back in soft shots that landed at the inrushing Richards' feet. During the first game, Richards hit three spectacular shots for winners. Unfortunately, he also hit five spectacular shots that either whapped into the net or sailed over the baseline. "Mr. Pfeiffer and Mr. Cranshaw lead one game to love," announced the umpire, Elwood R. Grandnoble, from the commanding height of the umpire's chair. Grandnoble, a tall, slender man of seventy-one with a flowing black toupee, was a notorious drinker and woman-chaser who had enjoyed a long, if checkered career involving stock fraud, income-tax irregularities, and influence peddling. But because he had played the game with occasional flashes of mediocrity for more than fifty years, and because he wore a black-dyed military mustache, a white blazer with a purloined Queen's Racquet Club emblem over the heart, and a white silk scarf, he was revered locally as "the grand old man of tennis." Cranshaw served first for the Tiddlingers. His underhand offering aggravated both Richards and Byznewski. His severely chopped ball to Richards would barely clear the net and bounce lifelessly no more than knee high. Richards would swoop up to it and hit a screaming forehand or backhand drive. Unfortunately, his return had to be high enough to rise over the net and low enough to land within the court. Under the immutable laws of physics, this trajectory of a ball traveling at something approaching the speed of light was an impossibility. Cranshaw favored Byznewski, on the other hand, with a sliced serve that bounced radically either left or right. The first two times, Byznewski, who had never seen such serves, guessed wrong. But after that, with the coolness of an old professional linebacker waiting to see which way the play was going, he would lie back, suddenly plunge and—swat!—the point would be over. Cranshaw promptly changed tactics and dished up his chopped serve to Byznewski, forcing the latter to simply push the ball back over the net. Cranshaw or Pfeiffer would then hit the ball softly to Richards's feet, no matter what the positions of the players on the court.

"It's all over but the racket flinging," said the Professor approvingly. "They are playing Richards."

And, indeed, Richards was growing increasingly errat- ic, not to mention apoplectic. ("It was bad enough," he confided afterward to Crestmarshian Coach Whizzer Whitman, "when I saw I was up against a couple of patty-cake ball pushers. I can't hit that kind of junk. I like to play with *real* tennis players, guys who put some pace on the ball. And then when I saw they were playing me instead of that dumb Byznewski . . . Well, I mean any *real* tennis player . . . I mean, Jesus!" At that point, he became too choked up to continue.)

"Point, set, and match," said Umpire Grandnoble, "to Mr. Cranshaw and Mr. Pfeiffer of the Tiddling Tennis Club, six games to four and six games to two."

Byznewski, grinning broadly, rushed to the net to shake Cranshaw's hand. "It's lucky I'm ambidextrous," said Cranshaw, examining his badly aching fingers as he walked off the court with Pfeiffer, "or I'd never play the violin again."

"You never played it before," said Pfeiffer.

"That's true," agreed Cranshaw cheerfully.

"The next event," announced Umpire Grandnoble, "will be the mixed doubles match. Representing the Tiddling Tennis Club will be Mr. and Mrs. Russell F. Conrad. Representing the Crestmarsh Racquet Club will be Mr. Garson Gersten and Mrs. J. Albert Moore."

"Thank God," said the Professor. "They aren't married to each other."

"But won't that give them the advantage?" asked Miss Merribuck.

"Precisely," agreed the Professor. "Given the Conrads' degree of compatability, they don't have a prayer of winning this one."

Miss Merribuck scratched her eyebrow. "You mean you want the Crestmarshians to win this time? But if we won, we'd keep the Dee Cup, and your troubles would be over, wouldn't they?"

"Many of them," agreed the Professor. "But none of Mr. Jackson's."

Miss Merribuck, smiling, placed her hand on his. "I don't know what you're up to exactly, John," she said, "but whatever it is, I'm glad."

"It is an extremely Machiavellian plot," said the Professor, "and, frankly, I'm quite pleased with it thus far."

"I wish you'd call me 'Merri,'" said Miss Merribuck.

Down on the court, the two teams were warming up. There seemed little to distinguish the one from the other. All four players exhibited classic strokes, or at least no glaring eccentricities. Mrs. Moore, a big-boned blonde, had the best tan, but Mrs. Conrad had the prettier dress. The Conrads won the spin and walked toward the shady side of the court, his arm about her waist.

"They seem quite compatible, don't they?" said Miss Merribuck.

"It won't last long," said the Professor confidently.

Actually, Conrad was giving his wife last-minute advice. "I want you to concentrate primarily on covering your alley," he said.

"And do you want me to bounce up and down all the time like that Candy Kupp did?" asked Mrs. Conrad.

"Oh, I wouldn't bother," said Conrad absently. That was his first mistake.

As Conrad had chosen the side, it was up to Gersten to decide whether to serve or receive. Gersten looked up into the sun and tossed the balls to Conrad. "We'll receive," he said. Conrad won his serve and Gersten his. Mrs. Conrad held. Then the Conrads broke Mrs. Moore, to take the lead three–one. That was just before the match ended.

Tension had been mounting on the Conrads' side of the net. Conrad was determined to play the same style of game he had played in the Club's mixed troubles tournament, bounding about the court and allowing Mrs. Conrad to take only an occasional forehand to her alley. But Mrs. Conrad was not as compliant a partner as Miss Kupp, the novice, and it was obvious to all from the set of her lips that her temper was mounting. "Stay on your own side of the bed," she muttered once when Conrad cut in front of her to miss a difficult low backhand volley on a ball which would have been an easy forehand drive for her. "Sorry," he said, putting very little feeling into it. With a commanding three–one lead, Conrad opened with a cannon-ball serve to Mrs. Moore's backhand. She barely managed to block it with her racket. It was the shot that won the match. The soft, high return landed just over the net between Mrs. Conrad and her inrushing husband. "Mine!" he cried as she was about to swing. Their rackets collided, and the ball skittered into the net.

"Damn," she said. "You could've killed me."

"I could now," he said grimly. "Didn't you hear me say 'Mine'?"

" 'Mine! Mine! Mine!' Who do you think you are, Attila the Hun?"

"Look, if you don't like the way I play—"

"Jesus, I love the way you play. But play on your own side of the God-damn court."

Up in the lounge, the Professor nodded complacently and said to Miss Merribuck, "Excuse me, it is now time for the *deus* to clamber out of the *machina*."

He made his way to the Tiddlingers' end of the grandstand and stopped before Judge Emmet (Judge) Fowler, who was sitting there in a white warm-up suit glumly watching the proceedings.

"Good morning, Professor," the Judge said with his customary courtly dignity. "I have been attempting to predict to myself who will win this knockdown, drag-out battle now in progress—Mr. Conrad or Mrs. Conrad."

"I think you must admit, Judge," said the Professor, "that it won't be the Tiddling Tennis Club. Possession of the Dee Cup will therefore hinge on the outcome of the singles match. So I must now ask you to carry out our agreement."

The Judge sighed. "Yes, I suppose you're correct."

The Professor removed a gold pocket watch from his yellowed flannel trousers and flicked it open. "Will it take long?" he asked. "I fear this match will be over more quickly than I had anticipated."

"I have always believed that justice should be swift, Professor," said the Judge as the two headed for the exit, "and mercy even swifter."

By now, the match had resumed, but it was no contest. Conrad sulkily delineated the boundaries on his side of the court as comprising the alley and as far as he could reach from therein without moving. Consequently, any shot hit down the middle was a likely winner. "Why didn't you get that?" Mrs. Conrad would demand.

"I didn't want to kill you, dear," he would reply sweetly, "in front of all these witnesses."

Forty minutes later, Umpire Grandnoble announced: "Game, set, and match to Mr. Gersten and Mrs. Moore of the Crestmarsh Racquet Club, six games to three and six games to love. In order to afford spectators and officials time to refresh themselves, there will be a brief intermission before the final and deciding match between Mr. Redford Head, representing the Crestmarsh Racquet Club, and Mr. Otis Otis III, representing the Tiddling Tennis Club." With that, Umpire Grandnoble clambered stiffly down from his stand and headed for the bar.

The phone rang in Miss Agnes's office. It was the Professor. "Is the mixed doubles over yet?" he asked.

"They are now sponging up the blood," said Miss Agnes.

"Damn," said the Professor. "Have they started the singles?"

"No, the umpire has called an intermission for refreshments."

"Grandnoble? Marvelous. Have Sam ply him with whisky sours, compliments of the house."

"Compliments of whose house? Some traditions are sacred, and one is that no one has ever had a free drink at the Tiddling Tennis Club."

"Put them on my bill. I need time. Someone sent the Judge's robe to the cleaners and to appear in court without one, he says, would defile the majesty of the law."

"Where are you? What are you up to?"

"I'm in the Judge's chambers, but . . . My God, the drapes! Why didn't I think of that before? Stall!"

Ten minutes later, an emergency session of the Criminal Court was called, Judge Emmet Fowler presiding. He presided in what appeared to be a black velvet toga and white tennis shoes. Standing before him to be arraigned on six counts of possession of marijuana and one count of parole violation was a somewhat bewildered-looking Beauregard Jackson.

"I understand, young man," said the Judge peering down from the bench, "that you move to dismiss the charges that have been brought against you on the grounds that your arrest violated your rights under the Fourth Amendment to the Constitution relative to illegal searches and seizures."

"I do?" said Jackson.

"You do," said the Judge sternly. "Let the record so show. And let the record also show that the court has given a great deal of thought to this grave Constitutional question and will rule on it as of Monday next."

"Who do?" said Jackson.

"I do," said the Judge. "Meanwhile, the court feels it would be most unjust to continue the incarceration of the defendant over the weekend and therefore releases him into the custody of his long-time mentor and benefactor, Mr. John Doe Roberts, pending his appearance before this court at ten o'clock Monday."

"Who that?" said Jackson.

"Court dismissed," said Judge Fowler.

The Professor, carrying a large, well-stuffed paper bag, grabbed Jackson's elbow and steered him down the aisle, out the courtroom door and into the marbled corridor.

"Hey, man," said Jackson. "You spring me?"

"No time," said the Professor, guiding Jackson out the main door and down the steps. "I'll explain in the police car."

Jackson took one look at the police car waiting at the curb and pulled back. "Oh, no," he said shaking his head. "I ain't never ridden in one of them, not when I could do the choosing."

"Think of it as a black-and-white taxicab," said the Professor.

"A cab it ain't," said Jackson adamantly.

"You force me to remind you that Judge Fowler released you in my custody," said the Professor impatiently. "Time is of the essence. And while you may feel uncomfortable riding in a police car, I am sure you will be more comfortable than you would be back in jail."

Jackson looked down at the Professor for a moment. "Shee-it," he said, and folded himself into the rear seat.

"To the Tiddling Tennis Club, please," the Professor

told the officer behind the wheel. "And, if my vernacular is correct, step on it!"

The officer reached forward to flick on red light and siren. "How come," he said out of the side of his mouth to his partner, "we get all the weirdos?"

"What the fuck's happening, man?" demanded Jackson, grabbing the door handle for support as the car squealed away from the curb.

"First of all," said the Professor, looking straight ahead, "I want you to know that it was I who caused the police to arrest you."

"You put the fuzz on my ass?" said Jackson, his eyes narrowing.

"Fuzz on your . . . Oh, yes. Yes, that's quite correct."

"Dudes get stuck for less," said Jackson angrily. "Why you do that?"

"Basically, I suppose my reason was selfish," said the Professor. "I wished you to play in the Dee Cup tournament. It was a matter of great importance to me."

"Shee-it. You think I'm laying my ass on the line for some ofay who put the pigs on me?"

"Yes, I think so. You see, there are other factors involved. I reasoned thus: sooner or later you would be arrested by the police. You would have no defense against the pending charges. Inevitably, you would be sent to the penitentiary. I therefore entered into negotiations with Judge Fowler. Fortunately, he feels strongly about retaining the Dee Cup, as he was a member of the doubles team that first helped win it thirty-three years ago. Unfortunately, I was forced to explain the unorthodox nature of your game. At first he was skeptical, but in the end, he became convinced. It was then he agreed that, if your presence became critical to the retention of the Dee Cup . . ."

"What the fuck you talking about, man?"

"He agreed that, if you win your match this afternoon, he will dismiss the charges pending against you, and your record will be clear."

A grin slowly spread over Jackson's features. "You mean I whup some honky and they spring my black ass? Man, that's what I call justice." He frowned. "Seems like you sure had a whole mess of 'ifs' in there."

The Professor nodded. "Yes, the major condition was that the Club would require your services to retain the Cup. I knew we would win the men's doubles match. The problem was the mixed doubles. Mr. and Mrs. Collums were a formidable team. If they, too, won, the tournament would have been over, and you would, I fear, have languished in jail."

"That's what I don't call no justice."

"Fortunately, all tennis players have weaknesses. I had studied Mr. Collums thoroughly over the years, and I believed I knew his. Immediately prior to his final match in the mixed troubles tournament, I imparted this information to his opponent, Mr. Conrad. He, in turn, instructed his attractive young partner on the proper tactic. It proved so effective that they not only defeated the Collumses but destroyed their marriage, and thus eliminated them from today's Dee Cup match."

"Man, you don't fool around. What did this chick do?"

"She simply bounced up and down on the balls of her feet."

"I don't dig."

"Mr. Collums' weakness was mammary glands," said the Professor with a smile.

"Who?"

"Tits, man."

A chuckle rumbled up out of Jackson's chest. "Hey!

Hey! Hey!" he cried over the wail of the siren. "You mighty hip, Prof." Again he frowned. "But seems like you had a couple more 'ifs' in there. I mean, like what if this honky dude whups me?"

"That possibility is infinitesimal. You will inevitably win both sets as long as your opponent, Mr. Redford Head, serves first. If Mr. Head wins the spin, he will elect to serve. He always does. Thus all you have to remember is this: *Should you win the spin, you must choose to receive.*"

The Professor said this with such intensity that Jackson scrunched up his shoulder. "Easy, man. I dig. He serves first."

"Sorry," apologized the Professor. "It is merely that not only this match but my entire life's work hinges on this point. But if you have it committed to memory . . ."

"That's one 'if' don't worry me none."

"One more 'if' that I hadn't included in my calculations," said the Professor, glancing at his pocket watch, "was if we arrive at the Club in time. That was why Judge Fowler was kind enough to offer us the services of these police officers. Which reminds me . . ." He opened the paper bag he had been carrying and proffered Jackson's tennis togs to him.

"You had best change your attire now, so that you will be prepared to take the field immediately upon your arrival, if we are not too late."

Jackson, grinning, waited until he had removed all his clothes before banging with his shoe on the wire mesh that separated them from the front seat. "Go, pigs, go!" he shouted happily at the top of his lungs.

The officer of the right turned, his eyes widening as they took in the scene in the rear. "Holy Mother of God!" he exclaimed.

THE TIDDLING TENNIS CLUB'S
GLORIOUS GAMBLE

Should you never cry out "Yea!" to the exciting challenge of an important match, you will never taste the bitter dregs of defeat.—Roberts's Rules of Order

At the Club, Otis and Head had been warming up for a half-hour, while Crestmarshian Coach Whizzer Whitman attempted to pry Umpire Grandnoble away from the bar. Head had arrived at the court first. He was a stocky, prematurely bald man, with a deeply tanned face and when he removed his ever-present tennis hat, a startlingly white pate. The total effect was reminiscent of a photographic negative. From his grim, almost ascetic visage, his pristine sweat bands on each wrist, his iron-creased shorts and shirt, his spotless white leather shoes, and the military manner in which he carried his three cover-enclosed rackets under his arm, it was clear he considered tennis to be the one and only true religion. A pace behind him came Coach Whitman, looking grand in long, white flannels and a white baseball cap, his paunch sheathed in a woolen tennis sweater. The Crestmarshians gave them a round of confident applause.

Otis, tall, knobby, blond, and looking, as always, somewhat disheveled, came bounding in a few minutes later, apologizing profusely for being late to an unsmiling Redford Head. The Tiddlingers applauded his entrance politely, their enthusiasm dimmed by the previous record of these encounters.

"It's like putting a puppy dog up against a tank," said Smeedle unhappily.

"Look at the bright side," said Doc Pritchgart. "It sure will cook the Professor's goose."

The two players commenced to warm up vigorously, the ball whistling back and forth between them. But as the minutes passed and Umpire Grandnoble failed to appear, both diminished the pace, each one walking more and more slowly to pick up errant balls in order to conserve energy.

In her office, Miss Agnes was conferring with Miss Merribuck. The two women had been somewhat reserved and overly polite with each other of late, but now the frowns they shared showed a common concern. Finally, Miss Merribuck nodded with determination and hurried up the stairs to the lounge. If her intent had been to deal further with Umpire Grandnoble, she was moments too late. He was at that very moment entering the arena to the ironic applause of the impatient crowd, his elbow being grasped like a tiller by Coach Whitman. Whitman steered him across the court and helped him up into his umpire's chair, help he quite obviously needed.

Once settled and secure, Grandnoble cleared his throat.

"This will be the final and deciding match . . ." he began in his most stentorian tone.

"You already said that," said Whitman.

"So I did," agreed Grandnoble. "Are the players ready? Play."

"We haven't spun for service yet," protested Head.

"So you haven't," agreed Grandnoble.

"Up or down?" said Head, spinning his racket.

"Up," said Otis as it clattered to the pavement.

"Down it is," said Head examining the emblem on the butt of the handle. "I'll serve first."

"I'll receive over there," said Otis, pointing to the shady side under the lounge windows.

"Mr. Otis will receive," said Grandnoble, waving vaguely, "over there."

At the bar, Miss Merribuck was talking to Sam. "Couldn't you have delayed him just a little longer?" she asked.

Sam, who was wiping a glass, shrugged. "Three whisky sours, compliments of the house," he said, smiling his inscrutable smile. "All very strong."

"We have to do something, Sam. It's for the Professor."

"Ah, the Professor." This time there was a hint of warmth in Sam's unfading smile. Misanthropy loves company.

"If we don't delay that match until he gets here . . ." She was twisting a paper napkin between her fingers. With a tug, she broke it in two. "O, damn! I don't know what will happen to him."

The vision of a machine gun raking the crowd flashed through Sam's head. That faded. He turned, selected a fresh bottle of crème de menthe from the shelf and placed it on the bar in front of Miss Merribuck, nodding at the new plate-glass windows behind her.

She looked at him blankly for a moment and then grinned. "So it was you the other night . . ."

Sam smiled his inscrutable smile. She swiveled on her barstool to reconnoiter. It was a good fifteen feet to the windows. The Tiddlingers were seated two deep in front of them, but their backs were to her as they watched the scene below. No one seemed to be looking at her but Sam. She hefted the bottle. The voice of Umpire Grandnoble drifted up: "Players ready? Play!"

Miss Merribuck clasped her lower lip firmly between her teeth, contracted her brows in a ferocious squint, hauled up the bottle, closed her eyes, and heaved. The brand new plate-glass window shattered, evoking traumatic cries from those who had been staring through it. The bottle arced downward, narrowly missing Otis, who was crouched to receive Head's serve, and exploded on the pavement into a fine mess of sticky green liqueur and glittering shards of glass.

It was never known precisely what caused Sam's mind to snap. (Perhaps he thought the revolution had come at last.) But snap it did. Over the bar he leapt with surprising agility, bounded across the lounge, and struck a pose in the now empty window frame. Raising a clenched fist to the upturned faces of those below, he shouted: "Death to the bosses!"

"Damn," said Herb Smeedle to Doc Pritchgart. "Now what the hell are we going to do with that commemorative platter we gave him?"

"Keep calm," cried Captain Alan (Buzz) Sawyer, USMC (retired), in the lounge, as he patted his pockets in search of his cigarette lighter.

"Arise ye prisoners of starvation!" shouted Sam, who appeared to be enjoying himself.

A police siren wailed up outside and died. "This is a

tennis club?" Head, always the purist, said in disgust.

"Workers of the world unite!" shouted Sam. "You have nothing to lose but your chains!"

At that point he was seized in a bear hug from behind by Sawyer. Sam wisely put up no resistance. For one thing, Sawyer outweighed him by sixty pounds; for another, he had exhausted his revolutionary vocabulary. He was again smiling inscrutably by the time a breathless Smeedle and Pritchgart arrived at the top of the stairs.

"Sam," said Doc Pritchgart, growling. "What on earth got into you?"

"Death to the bosses!" exclaimed Sam, smiling inscrutably.

"You maybe want me to tie him to a chair?" asked Captain Sawyer.

Smeedle looked shocked. "Not in the lounge, for heaven's sake. Let's take him down to Miss Agnes's office. She can call the police.

"Workers of the world unite," agreed Sam.

As they passed the Club entrance, they could see a police car at the curb through the iron-grilled glass door. Jackson, in his tennis togs, was standing on the sidewalk awaiting the Professor, who was conferring with the officer at the wheel.

"By golly, there's one now!" said Smeedle with surprise. "Bring him along."

Sawyer, who still had his arms around the unprotesting Sam, picked him up and carried him outside. "What the hell's this?" said the officer, who had been explaining to the Professor that accepting a twenty-five-cent tip was against Department regulations.

"This bartender of ours," said Smeedle, "has just revealed himself as a Red Chinese spy. He attempted to sabotage our Club lounge and foment a riot."

"Sam?" said the Professor incredulously.

"This true?" asked the officer.

Sam nodded cheerfully. "Arise ye prisoners of starvation," he said.

It was a good ten minutes before the two officers had enough names and details in their notebooks. They drove off with Sam sitting erect and regal in the back seat. His smile now seemed less inscrutable and more one of triumph.

"We sure do get the weirdos," said the officer at the wheel.

"Holy Mother of God!" agreed his partner.

By the time Jackson had fetched his racket from his locker and arrived at courtside, the crème de menthe mess had been almost entirely cleaned up. Head was doing limbering-up exercises at the far end, and Otis was leaning against the net post chatting with friends. When Jackson arrived with the Professor just behind him, the Tiddlingers burst forth in cheers and applause. Jackson dropped his racket and, grinning broadly, shook his clasped hands over his head in a prize-fighter's greeting. Coach Whitman, who had been looking forward to an easy win, correctly sensed that the Tiddlingers felt the cavalry had arrived. "What's this?" he said, intercepting the Professor and Jackson beneath Umpire Grandnoble's chair.

"This," said the Professor, "is Mr. Beauregard Jackson, who will represent the Tiddling Tennis Club in the final single's match."

"Oh, no you don't," said Whitman. "Otis will."

"We are making a substitution," said the Professor.

"What do you think this is, World Team Tennis? You can't make a substitution once play has begun."

"And has it begun?" asked the Professor, having been informed by Smeedle that it hadn't.

"Well, they've finished warming up. You can't expect another long delay while your new guy warms up."

"Mr. Jackson wouldn't dream of warming up. He loathes warming up. He is quite ready to play, thank you."

Sensing defeat, Whitman clutched at a straw. "Mr. Head won the spin. I hope you don't expect us to spin all over again. That wouldn't be fair."

"And what did Mr. Head elect to do?" inquired the Professor.

"I elected to serve," Head, who had joined the group, said sternly. "And I intend to."

"That is certainly acceptable," said the Professor magnanimously. "Now if the chair will announce its decision, we can commence play."

"What did the chair decide?" asked Umpire Grandnoble, who had been following the argument with an owlish expression.

"That Mr. Head will serve to Mr. Jackson," said the Professor.

"Mr. Head will serve to Mr. Jackson," announced Grandnoble as the two players took their positions. "Players ready?"

Head nodded curtly. "Yea-hey!" cried Jackson, whirling his racket above his head.

"Play!" said Grandnoble.

Head's first serve whistled past Jackson, who swung at it awkwardly, missing it by a good foot. The Crestmarshians clapped madly. The Tiddlingers fell silent.

"That's the Professor's ringer?" Doc Pritchgart asked Smeedle incredulously. "What's his bar bill up to now?"

Jackson, unconcerned, moved to the ad court to receive

Head's second service. This time, thanks to his reach, his dexterity, his quickness, and his inherent hand-eye coordination, he managed to meet the ball with his racket, returning a soft lob that Head had no trouble putting away. Head won the first game, to a mixture of applause and apprehensive silence, at love.

"Now?" Miss Merribuck inquired of the Professor, whom she had joined at courtside.

The Professor, who was marking a place in the USLTA rule book as the two players changed sides, nodded. "Now," he said. "By the way, were you there when Sam threw that bottle?"

"He didn't throw it," she said, looking down at her clasped hands. "I did."

"Marvelous," said the Professor. "Now you're involved, too."

She looked up at him. "Yes," she said simply. Then she scratched her eyebrow. "But I feel guilty about Sam. Do you think I should confess?"

The Professor shook his head. "Emphatically not," he said. "Sam has gone to a far better place, I know."

The players had taken the court again. "Mr. Head leads one game to love," announced Umpire Grandnoble in his most mellifluous baritone. "Mr. Jackson will serve. Mr. Jackson? Are you prepared to serve, Mr. Jackson? Mr. Jackson?"

Jackson was crouched a good four feet behind the service line, racket in one hand, ball in the other, a broad grin on his face. "I'm ready, Ump. You ask him if he's ready."

"Are you ready, Mr. Head?" asked Grandnoble.

"Ready," said Head, eyeing Jackson doubtfully. "I guess."

Jackson inhaled deeply, took one giant stride forward,

and launched himself from the service line. As he approached perigee, he tossed up the ball. At perigee, his toes were four feet, his right hand thirteen feet, and the head of his racket sixteen feet above the court. His racket struck the ball squarely, sending it hurtling downward at a 45° angle. It bounced in Head's service court and sailed far over his open mouth and rolled-back eyes, striking the second-floor window of the Club lounge with a loud "thonk."

Whizzer Whitman was on his feet before Jackson had landed in a crouch half-way to the net. "Foot fault!" cried Whitman angrily.

"Foot fault!" echoed Head indignantly.

"Foot fault?" said Jackson. "What for's a foot fault?"

Umpire Grandnoble stroked his mustache uncertainly with thumb and forefinger. "Foot fault," he agreed.

The Professor sauntered to the umpire's chair with Whizzer Whitman in hot pursuit. "Mr. Umpire," said the Professor, bowing slightly and holding up a copy of the USLTA rule book, "may I draw your attention to Rule Six, entitled 'Delivery of Service.' And I quote: 'The service shall be delivered in the following manner. Immediately before commencing the serve, the Server shall stand with both feet at rest behind the base line. The Server shall then project the ball by hand into the air in any direction, and before it hits the ground, shall strike it with his racket, and the delivery shall be deemed to have been completed at the moment of the impact of the racket and the ball.' "

Whizzer Whitman scratched his brow. Grandnoble scratched his mustache, Head scratched the lobe of his left ear. Jackson, leaning against the net post and smiling beatifically, scratched his crotch. Grandnoble leaned down with great dignity, took the book from the Professor, slowly read the passage aloud once again in his mellifluous voice, and handed it back.

"Mr. Jackson," said the Professor, "unarguably stood, immediately before the serve, with both feet at rest behind the base line. While it is true that, following the serve, his feet landed inside the base line, they did so only after the impact of his racket with the ball, and therefore after—and I must stress, *after*—the delivery of service was deemed to have been completed. Once he has completed the delivery of his service, he is, of course, entitled to place his feet anywhere he wishes within the confines of the court."

Mr. Grandnoble looked down at the book for guidance, up to the heavens for guidance, pursed his lips, and finally announced his decision. "Fifteen–love," said Mr. Grandnoble.

"Yea-hey!" said Jackson.

From that point, as the Professor had predicted, the outcome was inevitable. Head made a supreme effort, standing at the boundary of his service court and attempting to hit Jackson's startling serves just as they bounded. This tactic, however, required not a supreme effort, but a superhuman one, and Jackson won his serve at love. The match proceeded inexorably, with each player holding service. Occasionally, the receiver would garner a point with a flukey mis-hit, and once Jackson not only returned the ball, but rushed the net, leaped high in the air, and put Head's ball away with a creditable smash. This drew the only round of applause of the day. One–all, two–one, two–all, three–two . . . With Head leading six games to five, Jackson served to make it six–all.

"The players will play a sudden-death tie breaker," intoned Umpire Grandnoble. "The first player to reach five points will win. Each player will serve two points in rotation. In the event the score is tied at four points all, the last player to serve will serve the ninth and deciding point. Mr. Head will serve first."

"Wouldn't you like to serve first?" Head asked Jackson, generously holding forth the balls.

"Man, I wouldn't dee-prive you of the honor," said Jackson, grinning. "Not for all the grass in Acapulco."

"Maybe they should spin for it," suggested Whizzer Whitman.

The Professor was slowly on his way to the umpire's chair, like a baseball manager heading for the mound. "Unfortunately, Mr. Umpire," he said, "the rules require that the players serve in rotation. And, as Mr. Jackson served the last game of the set, it is obviously Mr. Head's duty to serve the first two points of the tie breaker."

Whitman declined to argue the point. Instead, he asked for a ruling on who would serve the first game of the second set.

"Well . . ." said Grandnoble.

"Mr. Head, of course," interrupted the Professor. "Mr. Jackson served the final game of the first set."

Head reluctantly served first, winning the first two points. Jackson evened it at two–all. Head made it four–two. Jackson tied it up at four–all and prepared to serve the deciding point. From his position well behind the line, he held up the ball. "Here it comes, baby!" he cried. And this time, with victory in the air, he put enough extra effort in his swing to send the bounding ball soaring over the clubhouse roof. He took the second ball from his pocket and slammed it straight down on the court like a wide receiver spiking a football following a touchdown. He then did a little shuffling dance that has become a triumphant ritual on the gridiron and tried to leap into the Professor's arms. As the Professor was hugging Miss

Merribuck at the moment, all three went down in a tangled heap. The applause of the Tiddlingers died. "This is tennis?" said Smeedle to Doc Pritchgart.

"Point, tie breaker, and first set to Mr. Jackson," said Umpire Grandnoble looking at an indeterminate point somewhere above the Club's wall. "Mr. Head will serve to begin the second set."

Head thought this over, carefully encased his racket in its cover, zipped it, and walked off the court.

"Mr. Head defaults," said Grandnoble without surprise. "Match to Mr. Jackson of the Tiddling Tennis Club. Will everyone please rise for the presentation of the Dee Cup."

The Crestmarshians rose, gathered their things, and headed for the exit en masse. "Say-hey!" Jackson called after them. "Don't none of you want to press my flesh?" He turned to the Professor. "My, my," he said, shaking his head in mock sadness at this appalling lack of sportsmanship, "just 'cause I won their fucking cup . . ."

"It's the way you won it," said the Professor. "All tennis players are purists," he said, smiling, "when it comes to other tennis players, that is. And they are particularly so when they lose."

"That more honky shit?"

The Professor nodded. "Certainly," he said. "And that is precisely what you demonstrated to them with your unorthodox serve. This is why they are somewhat resentful."

Bo Jackson's slow, rumbling laugh exploded. He grabbed the Professor's wrist, turned his hand over palmside up and slapped it with his own. "Man, you really offed them dudes!" he said. "Outta sight. Outta sight. The Bo-joe-lay, she is on me."

The three made their way up the stairs to the lounge. The Tiddlingers they passed offered brief congratulations and turned away, as though embarrassed. Jackson eyed their retreating backs, cocked his head, and grinned. "Seems like you kind of offed them mothers, too, huh, Prof?" he said.

"Well, I fear they also are tennis players," said the Professor. "But they'll come around. They'll want you for a partner in doubles as soon as you've developed an all-around game to complement your serve."

"I been thinking," said Jackson, pursing his lips. "Ain't no way I'm gonna be making big bread fooling around with no tennis racket."

The Professor briefly bowed his head, eyes closed. "I confess that I misled you when I spoke of top professionals earning more than a hundred thousand dollars annually," he said, now looking squarely at Jackson. "They indeed do. But you indeed won't."

"I don't understand," said Miss Merribuck. "With his unreturnable serve . . ."

"Mr. Jackson has correctly calculated that once knowledge of his unreturnable serve becomes widespread, he would win only fifty per cent of his matches, depending on the spin of the racket, as his opponents would invariably elect to receive," said the Professor. "Thus, on the average, he would progress beyond the first round of any tournament only half the time, and the odds against his reaching the finals would be astronomical."

"But with practice . . ." said Miss Merribuck.

"To be a top professional, one must practice eight hours a day," said the Professor, "from the age of eight."

"Crazy, man," said Jackson.

The Professor turned to him. "With your athletic ability and coordination, you could be a very good A player in a couple of years, but that's all," he said. "I'm truly sorry I misled you."

Jackson looked down at him a moment, then put his

hand on his shoulder and grinned. "Hey, man, no sweat," he said. "I had me a ball." He turned and rapped an ashtray on the bar to attract the attention of Buzz Sawyer, who had gamely volunteered to fill in for the absent Sam. "*Garçon,*" he said, "hustle us up a bottle of Bo-joe-lay, one of them big mothers."

At the domino table, Doc Pritchgart looked at Herb Smeedle and nodded grimly.

"Wouldn't you rather do it?" asked Smeedle hopefully.

"You're the President," said Doc Pritchgart.

"It's a lonely, agonizing job, being President," said Smeedle with a sigh. He rose slowly and waddled over to Jackson. "I just wondered if you knew that wine costs three-fifty a bottle?" he said. "I mean I didn't know whether you knew that or not, if you see what I mean. But it's kind of important because I'm afraid I've got some bad news about your athletic scholarship."

Jackson looked down on him with a peculiar expression. "Likewise," he said.

"I mean you were granted the scholarship so that you could play for the Dee Cup. I mean it was the Professor's idea. And I'm sure it's been a wonderful experience for a young man to have enjoyed . . ."

"Say-hey!" agreed Jackson.

". . . the companionship of the Club members. The . . ."

"Real brothers," agreed Jackson.

". . . time has come, however . . ."

"If you say what I think you're going to say, Herb," said Miss Merribuck angrily. "I'll kill you."

". . . regretfully to inform you that . . ." Smeedle paused, his hearing only now catching up with his talking. He looked up at Jackson. "Likewise?" he asked. "Likewise what?"

"Likewise I got some bad news for you," Jackson said somberly, clasping Smeedle's limp right hand in both of his. "Now I ain't saying this here Club ain't the finest club I ever been a member of. And I ain't saying that each and every brother here ain't a credit to his race. And I ain't saying tennis ain't a wonderful, wonderful game. But, truth is, I done decided to ree-sign my membership."

"Resign?" Smeedle looked stunned. "But you can't resign. Nobody resigns from the Tiddling Tennis Club, not unless they're moving away forever. You aren't moving away forever, are you?" he asked, hopefully.

"No way."

"Then why would you want to resign?" Smeedle's voice was rising·in disbelief. "Why would anybody ever want to resign?"

"Better I don't say," said Jackson, shaking his head, his expression one of deep concern for Smeedle's sensibilities.

"But you *have* to. Everybody's going to ask. What will I tell them?"

"You just say I figured to be happier with my own kind."

"Well, I could tell them that. But what about tennis? You could be an A player in no time."

Jackson nodded. "Yeah, man," he said, "Just think: me, Bo Jackson, an A player!" He paused to sigh a sigh of cosmic regret. "Sure is a fucking shame I ain't got the time."

Before Smeedle could say another word, Jackson released his hand, slapped him on the shoulder, and beamed down at him. "But don't you fret none," he said, consolingly. "Bet my ass you find some little kid, he be happy to take my place."

Jackson turned and headed for the stairs. The other

three watched him, Smeedle open-mouthed, Miss Merri-buck frowning, and the Professor smiling. "He forgot this," said the Professor, picking up Jackson's racket, which was leaning against the bar. "He might want it as a souvenir."

The Professor caught up with Jackson by the front door. The two stood looking at each other for a moment. The Professor tucked the racket under one arm and slowly held out both hands, palms upward. "Hey, Bo, man," he said, "you sure done offed them mothers."

Up rumbled Jackson's laugh as he slapped the Profes-sor's palms. "My dear Professor," he said in a fair imitation of an upper-class British accent, as he accepted the racket with a courtly bow, "you are truly a credit to your race."

In the lounge, Smeedle had finished recounting his adventure to an incredulous Doc Pritchgart. "Pull your-self together," the latter said. "If a story like that gets around, it's not going to reflect any credit on the Club."

"What gets me most," said Smeedle, "is that I think he honestly believes he's better than we are."

"And fifteen for three" said Doc Pritchgart, taking advantage of Smeedle's condition to move his peg for-ward five holes. "You've got to be kidding."

THE TIDDLING TENNIS
THEOREM REVEALED

The day will inevitably dawn when you ask yourself why you are devoting so much of your time to attempting to hit a ball over a net between the confines of painted lines. The proper response is: "What the hell else would I be doing?"
—Roberts's Rules of Order

"Did you give him his racket?" asked Miss Merribuck when the Professor rejoined her in the lounge.

"I did," said the Professor. He was looking most pleased with himself. "I doubt that he really wants it, though. Isn't it odd that he should be the first to comprehend and apply my Tiddling Tennis Theorem?"

"Marvelous," agreed Miss Merribuck. But she appeared apprehensive. "Come sit down." She took his hand and led him to a table by the window. With the tournament over, the lounge was crowded with Tiddlingers advancing and retreating in the match-arranging ritual. ("Sorry, I think I already have a game.

However . . .") She released his hand to sit down and took it again when he joined her. "What will you do now, John?" she asked.

"Do?" he said. "Actually I hadn't given the matter much thought. I suppose I shall follow the dictates of my theorem, emulate Mr. Jackson, and resign. After all, my work here is complete."

"But what will you do? Do you have any money?"

"Oh, yes. Mother left me some. I think it's in a suitcase in my closet. Mother never did trust banks."

"But you said you took this job because you had to work for a living."

"I meant as a reason for living. It seemed as good a reason as any."

"And now you have no reason? John, you're not thinking of . . . of . . ."

The Professor smiled. "The trouble with suicide, I have always said, is that it limits your options. No, having mastered tennis, I suppose I shall return to philosophy. I'm writing a book, you know, about my narrow field of specialization. It's entitled 'The Nature of Man, the Essence of God, and the Meaning of Life.' I'm proud to say that I'm already up to page seven."

Miss Merribuck looked at him thoughtfully. "You know that I'm in love with you, don't you?"

The Professor withdrew his hand from hers. "Possibly," he said.

"I think you're in love with me, too, aren't you?"

"I'm striving desperately to avoid it."

"Damn! You can't go through life avoiding everything forever."

"I almost did." The Professor had formed a church and steeple with his interlocked fingers. He looked down upon his work intently. "In order to justify such conduct,

I had to prove my theorem. But in order to prove my theorem, I had to become involved." He hunched his shoulders. "I was forced to *use* people. No one should do that."

"Everybody uses everybody else. It's called human relationships."

The Professor took a deep breath. "As you said, if you must use people, you should at least return them in as good condition as you found them."

"You did, didn't you?"

"Mr. Jackson, possibly. Certainly not the Collumses."

"Don't be silly. A marriage that can't survive a tennis match can't be much of a marriage."

"There aren't many," agreed the Professor.

Miss Merribuck took his hand again. "I think I see. You're afraid of using me, aren't you? But I'd like being used. It would make me feel useful. I haven't felt useful in so long."

The Professor remained silent, head bowed. Miss Merribuck finally squeezed his hand and released it. "And what about your theorem?" she said brightly. "Will you publish it?"

"Publish it?" The Professor looked up, startled. "Good heavens no! Why would I do that?"

"But after all these years of work . . . Do you want it to go for nothing?"

The Professor shrugged. "Once the theorem was proved, it automatically became absolutely valueless."

"I'm not so sure," said Miss Merribuck. "What if you posted it on the bulletin board?"

"But what good . . ."

Miss Merribuck merely arched her eyebrows and swept the room with her hand, palm up, as though politely gesturing someone to the door.

"Oh," said the Professor. "Oh, I see what you mean. Once they comprehend my theorem, they will have to apply it. And then . . ."

"Don't look now," said Smeedle nervously. "But the Professor's grinning at us."

"And ten for two," said Doc Pritchgart, relentlessly moving his peg three holes forward. "You've got to be kidding."

The Professor had now clasped Miss Merribuck's hand in both of his. "Merri, that's a delightful idea," he said, his voice vibrant with excitement. "This place will topple like a house of cards."

Miss Merribuck was smiling at him. "I never really quite believed it existed anyway, did you?" she asked.

The Professor shook his head, smiling back. "It is most improbable, when you stop to think about it."

"When will you do it?"

"Now, I suppose. I shall just stop to post the theorem on my way out. Miss Agnes should have a large sheet of cardboard, a ruler, and a—"

"John, please take me with you."

Again he removed his hands. "You know I can't, Merri. If you understood my theorem, you would understand why."

"Damn it, it's obvious I do understand your theorem. What else have we been talking about?"

"Yes, I see. That was dense of me." He frowned. "And do you accept it?"

She shrugged. "Sure, why not?"

"But it doesn't apply only to tennis, you know."

"I know. All your little maxims—your theorem—the whole ball of wax applies to life itself, doesn't it?"

"But if you accept that, then what is the point of—"

"You accept that," she said firmly, "and then you go on from there."

"On?" He was still frowning. "On where?"

"You enjoyed getting involved with Bo Jackson, and the police, and the judge, and all that, didn't you?"

He thought for a moment. "Yes, I suppose I did," he finally said reluctantly.

"And you're enjoying the thought of posting your theorem and bringing down this whole silly place, aren't you?"

He smiled faintly. " 'Relishing' would be more the word for it," he said.

"Then I have one more last and final maxim for you." Now she was smiling, too, but it was more a smile of triumph.

"How odd," said the Professor. "I had always supposed that my theorem, once proved, was the be-all and end-all. But do go ahead."

"It isn't whether you win or lose," said Miss Merribuck slowly, "it's how much you enjoy the game."

Neither she nor the Professor was ever seen within the confines of the Tiddling Tennis Club again. It was almost as though they had ceased to exist. Nor, despite the hopeful expectations of those two iconoclasts, did the posting of the Professor's theorem have the slightest effect whatsoever on that venerable institution. "Good riddance," was Doc Pritchgart's only comment when he read it. The other members appeared either puzzled or bemused, as though faced with some arcane joke. The directors swiftly replaced Sam with an Irishman whose favorite expressions were "faith and begorrah," when sober, and "holy horseshit" after five p.m. The Professor's position was taken by a methodical, young, former German junior champion, much to the delight of the lady members, whom he methodically proceeded to seduce in alphabetical order.

The sole evidence that the Professor had ever existed at all was the placard. As no one else wanted it, Miss Agnes removed it from the bulletin board the following day and now treasures it among her souvenirs. It looks like this:

THE TIDDLING TENNIS THEOREM

TENNIS
IS
ABSURD
